W.V.

He pulled her against him.

She felt his strong arms encircle her and she didn't resist. When she'd agreed to come today, she'd known what might happen. Since their kiss yesterday, it had been inevitable.

But this time she wasn't a naive girl. She was an experienced woman. She was too honest to pretend reluctance, too filled with desire to be coy. And so she pressed her body against his and felt the soft, curling hair on his chest where his gray shirt was unbuttoned.

She wanted him. God, how she wanted him. She had wanted him all this time and been foolish enough to try to deny it. Now, she couldn't deny any of her feelings for him...the tenderness, the hunger, the need.

Dear Reader:

Romance offers us all so much. It makes us "walk on sunshine." It gives us hope. It takes us out of our own lives, encouraging us to reach out to others. Janet Dailey is fond of saying that romance is a state of mind, that it could happen anywhere. Yet nowhere does romance seem to be as good as when it happens *here*.

Starting in February 1986, Silhouette Special Edition is featuring the AMERICAN TRIBUTE—a tribute to America, where romance has never been so wonderful. For six consecutive months, one out of every six Special Editions will be an episode in the AMERICAN TRIBUTE, a portrait of the lives of six women, all from Oklahoma. Look for the first book, *Love's Haunting Refrain* by Ada Steward, as well as stories by other favorites—Jeanne Stephens, Gena Dalton, Elaine Camp and Renee Roszel. You'll know the AMERICAN TRIBUTE by its patriotic stripe under the Silhouette Special Edition border.

AMERICAN TRIBUTE—six women, six stories, starting in February.

AMERICAN TRIBUTE—one of the reasons Silhouette Special Edition is just that—Special.

The Editors at Silhouette Books

PAMELA WALLACE
All My Love, Forever

Silhouette Special Edition

Published by Silhouette Books New York

America's Publisher of Contemporary Romance

SILHOUETTE BOOKS
300 East 42nd St., New York, N.Y.   10017

ISBN: 0-373-09311-X

First Silhouette Books printing May 1986

America's Publisher of Contemporary Romance

Printed in the U.S.A.

Books by Pamela Wallace

Silhouette Special Edition

Love with a Perfect Stranger #63
Dreams Lost, Dreams Found #102
Tears in the Rain #255
All My Love, Forever #311

Silhouette Desire

Come Back, My Love #13

Silhouette Intimate Moments

Fantasies #24
Cry for the Moon #48
Promises in the Dark #58
Scoundrel #83

PAMELA WALLACE

is a professional writer who has written for TV and magazines, besides having written numerous works of fiction. Her spirited characters come alive on every page as she weaves thought-provoking stories of true-to-life romance. Ms. Wallace lives in Fresno, California.

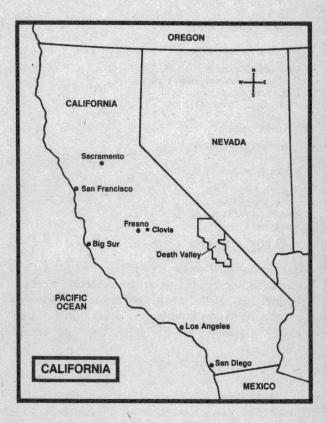

Prologue

Clovis, California, Spring, 1961

The last bell of the day rang shrilly, and students poured out of the classrooms of Clovis High School. Outside Mr. Malone's seniors' civics class, Marcia Pieroni stopped to talk to Caroline Cummings.

"Did you hear the latest about Sue Krauss and Rafe Marin?"

Caroline's golden brown eyes were lit by amusement. "No, but judging by your tone, it must be pretty good."

"Boy, is it! A sheriff's deputy caught them parked up in the foothills and took her home. Her parents were furious that their precious little cheerleader would be involved with the son of a Mexican-American gardener. She's grounded for about ninety-nine years."

Caroline shrugged and moved her books from one arm to the other. "That isn't exactly hot news, Marcia. Rafe's made out with half the girls in this school."

"Yeah, word has it that Sue wasn't wearing a thing when the deputy caught them."

"Nothing?"

"Not a stitch." Marcia's voice lowered to a conspiratorial whisper as other students milled around them. "Do you think they actually did anything?"

"How would I know? Anyway, enough of Rafe Marin. Want to come over tomorrow and study for the civics test?"

"Caroline Cummings, don't try to pretend you're above juicy gossip."

"I'm not pretending anything. I'm just bored with Rafe and his endless reputation."

"Bored? How can you possibly be bored with him?"

"It's easy. He's a jerk."

"He's also a hunk. Oh, my God, there he is!"

From the end of the hall, Rafe Marin walked toward them. Caroline didn't want to stare at him, but she couldn't help herself. Somehow he compelled attention. She had to admit that he was, indeed, a hunk. He wasn't exactly handsome, but there was something about him. He had the aura of the forbidden, the dangerous. His lithe, lean body moved with an unstudied grace.

As he passed Caroline and Marcia, he glanced at them for a moment, then moved on. But in his gray eyes was something Caroline couldn't quite fathom—something intriguing.

When he was gone, Marcia went on, "I'd climb into a back seat with him any day."

"Marcia!"

"Hey, I was only joking. Sort of."

"Nice girls don't climb into back seats with anyone, let alone a guy like Rafe."

"I know, I know," Marcia responded irritably. Then she added with a sigh, "Nice girls also don't have any fun."

Caroline smiled ruefully. "True. Well, I've gotta go, my mom will be waiting out front to pick me up. Are you gonna come over tomorrow to study?"

"Sure, why not? I don't have anything more exciting to do."

"Okay. See you then."

But as she walked outside, it wasn't the upcoming civics test that was on her mind. It was Rafe. Unlike Caroline, he wasn't a virgin, she was sure. He'd explored the mystery of the forbidden subject of sex. What was it like, she wondered? What would it be like with him?

Such thoughts were all wrong, she knew, and she tried to banish them from her mind. But they stayed at the back of her thoughts, nagging and insistent. At seventeen, she was as innocent and naive as a very sheltered, strictly reared banker's daughter should be. Extremely shy, she had dated very little, and then only with boys who were friends, whose parents knew her parents.

Yet while she accepted the rigid limitations placed on her behavior, she couldn't help wondering what she was missing. Whatever it was, she sensed Rafe could supply it in abundance.

The week passed by without any other events to stir the fires of young imaginations. However, one day late in the next week, Caroline found herself sitting in the stands of the Clovis High School stadium, watching a track meet between Clovis and Fresno High. Down on the dirt track, a group of young men dressed in running shorts and T-shirts took their mark. One of them was Rafe.

Even from a distance, it was easy to pick him out from the others. His black hair shone ebony in the bright sunlight and his skin was the mellow brown of caramel. Though he wasn't big, there was a wiry strength to his body, evident in the sinewy muscles in his arms and legs.

When the starter's pistol sounded, the group took off in a staggered profile as each ran in his own lane all the way around the circular track. Rafe was near the front and Caroline watched, enchanted, as he moved with the powerful grace of a big cat.

While all the young men ran hard, Caroline sensed something different about Rafe. He seemed driven. Whether he was trying to prove something to himself or to everyone else, she didn't know. But she could tell by the way his muscles strained, and the intense expression on his face, that he was going all out, holding nothing back.

Somehow, she found herself rooting for him. Silently she urged, "Come on, Rafe, you can do it, leave them all behind."

And he did. With one long stride after another, he caught and passed the leaders. It was his broad, hard chest that touched the ribbon at the finish line first.

As he came to a shaky stop, then bent over, gasping for breath, Caroline realized what must be driving him. Not one of the other runners, who were all anglo, went over to congratulate him.

Yet something in his proud attitude as he straightened up suggested that it didn't matter. Even if they wouldn't accept him, he had the pleasure of knowing he had beaten them. He might be a Mexican-American gardener's son, as Marcia had said, but he had just run the people who looked down on him into the ground.

Then Rafe glanced into the stands. His eyes locked with Caroline's for a long, long moment before she finally tore hers away. When she looked back, he was walking away.

A few minutes later, Caroline was walking out of the stadium when she heard a husky voice call her name. Turning, she came face to face with Rafe. He had showered and changed into jeans and a shirt. His dark hair glistened wetly and had obviously been hurriedly combed.

"I saw you in the stands," he began easily.

Caroline's innate shyness was even more acute than usual. "Yes," she murmured, not quite meeting his look. "Congratulations on winning."

"Thanks."

Though they had been in some of the same classes together all through high school, they'd never talked. This was their first real conversation, and Caroline found it very awkward.

Desperately searching for something to say, she went on, "You're a very good runner."

Rafe smiled. "Thanks again."

He didn't seem to feel any awkwardness, she thought irritably. But then he had a great deal more experience in dealing with the opposite sex than she did.

"Well, goodbye," she finished and started to turn away.

"Will you go out with me tonight?"

The casual invitation stopped her abruptly. Turning back to face him, she said in an even voice, "I thought you were dating Sue."

"Not anymore." There wasn't a trace of embarrassment in his voice or his look as he watched her. "Well?" he went on.

Amusement glinted in his silvery gray eyes, and she realized that he found her awkwardness funny. Which only deepened her chagrin.

"I'm busy tonight," she finally lied.

"What about next Saturday?"

She was caught off guard by his persistence. Clearly, he didn't intend to be put off easily. She couldn't tell him she was dating someone else, because Clovis was so small he would know that she wasn't involved with anyone in particular. Besides, lying wasn't something she felt comfortable doing.

What could she say? she wondered. "I don't want to go out with you." But that wasn't the truth. Actually, she was surprised at how much she did want to go out with him, in spite of his reputation. Or because of it, a tiny voice deep inside slyly suggested.

When she didn't answer, he went on, "Unless your parents don't want you dating their gardener's son."

His tone was flip, but his eyes betrayed anger behind the words.

Looking into them, Caroline knew she couldn't hurt his feelings by admitting he was right. Such a put-down would hurt rather than anger him, she had no doubt, though she couldn't have said how she knew.

Gathering her courage, she met his look. "I'll go out with you. My address is 111 W. Anderson. What time will you be by?"

"Seven o'clock?"

"Fine."

"Good. See you then."

He walked away without a backward glance.

What on earth have I done? Caroline asked herself.
But she knew the answer quite well. She'd just agreed to
go out with the most notorious young man at Clovis
High.

Chapter One

A huge banner across one wall of the high school gym read CLOVIS HIGH SCHOOL, CLASS OF 1961. Seeing it, Caroline Turner felt bemused. Had it really been twenty-five years since she'd last been here? she asked herself.

She didn't feel like that much time had passed, and she certainly didn't look it. She was still slender and pastel-colored, a honey-blonde with golden eyes and porcelain fine skin.

But there was nothing of the china doll about her. The years had lain a subtle yet unmistakable character over the soft beauty. There was a firmness in the pointed chin, and the wide, full mouth wasn't the type to simper. There was courage there, too, and intelligence, qualities that had only been vaguely apparent in the teenage girl she had been when she had last walked into this gym.

"I feel seventeen again," her friend Marcia said with a grin. "Like the entrance to this gym is a time tunnel and when I come through it I'm no longer a mature woman. I'm a kid again and can be silly and make a fool of myself if I want."

Caroline's laughter was soft and indulgent. "We did make fools of ourselves, didn't we? But it didn't matter. All that mattered was having fun."

Marcia cocked her head to one side and her deep-blue eyes, a startling contrast to her black hair, eyed Caroline shrewdly. "Now, aren't you glad you came, after all?"

Caroline shot her a wry grin. "Yes, but don't press the issue." Suddenly, concern clouded her tawny eyes. "Marcia, are you sure—"

"Yes, I'm sure," Marcia broke in, answering the question before Caroline could even finish it. "He won't be here. He hasn't come to any of the reunions. Just like you. Now, relax and enjoy yourself."

Around them, dozens of other members of the class of '61 mingled. They talked, laughed, and not very subtly appraised how well they'd each handled the passing years.

"Oh, look," Marcia exclaimed, "There's Danny Thayer. He was on the reunion committee with me. I've got to talk to him about the cocktail party at the Hilton tomorrow night."

Her round face with its youthful smattering of golden freckles was split by a wide grin. "I can't wait to say 'I told you so' to him. He thought it would be dumb to have this dance here in the old gym. But everyone seems to really be enjoying it. I'll be right back."

She left, and Caroline moved over to a relatively quiet corner. She'd never entirely outgrown the shyness that had plagued her in high school, and she wasn't quite ready yet to make small talk with people she hadn't seen in so many years. Instead, she watched the milling crowd that was growing thicker by the minute, picking out familiar faces and remembering experiences they'd shared.

She spotted the girl who'd been valedictorian. Wearing a stunning black lace dress, she looked surprisingly chic for someone who had once had no time to worry about her appearance.

And across the room was the boy who'd taken Caroline to the junior prom. There had been no romance between them, just the comfortable friendship of two kids who'd grown up next-door to each other. Caroline had gone with him because he didn't have the courage to invite anyone else.

He had been skinny and awkward then. Now, he was quite handsome and quietly confident. Caroline wasn't surprised to see a stunning blonde on his arm. Obviously, he'd come a long way from that gangly, insecure boy. He was definitely someone she'd like to do some catching up with this evening, she thought.

On the dais, a small combo was warming up. The tune was vaguely familiar yet the title was somehow elusive.

For a moment, Caroline listened intently, trying to remember. And then it came to her.

"Heart and Soul."

In a rush of memory the words came, too.

Heart and soul,
I fell in love with you,
now I know what one embrace can do,
magic,
we fell in love in the night....

Suddenly, the name she'd avoided mentioning out loud came unbidden into her thoughts.

Rafe.

Rafe had held her while they danced to that song. The leashed strength in his lean, hard young body had sent shock waves of desire racing through her. He'd whispered the lyrics in her ear, his breath blowing warm and sweet against her cheek. She had trembled in his arms, as deep inside her something wild and wonderful happened.

The memory of that intense passion was as vivid as if she were with him at that moment. As if she was staring into those quicksilver eyes....

With a start, she realized she was staring into those gray eyes. Across the crowded room, her eyes locked with his as the lights dimmed and the band began playing "Heart and Soul" in earnest.

Oh, my God, she thought desperately.

Her entire body went rigid at the unexpected—the unthinkable. Then, all rational thought was extinguished as she watched him slowly make his way through the crowd toward her.

From a distance, and in the dim light, he looked startlingly the same. The leanness of his body made him seem taller than his five feet, ten inches. His black hair was thick and shiny, his skin a deep olive. Only his eyes were light, the pure, clear gray of steel or a silver coin.

As he came closer Caroline forced herself to stand her ground, though what she wanted to do more than anything was to turn and flee. Enough adrenaline was pumping through her to make her flight swift.

But she knew she couldn't run away. She had tried it for years, and it hadn't worked. She knew she had to stand her ground and face this man, no matter how painful it was to do so. Digging her nails into the palms of her hands which hung rigidly at her sides, she waited.

He stopped right in front of her. She was no longer aware of the crowd surrounding them. There was only her and Rafe.

Seen up close, he didn't look so uncannily the same. After all, she realized, he was forty-two now, not seventeen. There were flecks of silver at his temples. His face, while unlined, was harder, more mature. It was still not quite perfect enough to be called handsome, yet it was very attractive.

He looked her up and down slowly, almost lazily, in the disturbingly frank way she remembered so well. The years certainly hadn't humbled him, she thought. He was every bit the thoroughly sensual male he'd been as a high school senior, with a hint of danger in those quicksilver eyes that was highly erotic. If anything, he was even more sensual, for now he was a man, not a boy.

When he spoke, his voice was deeper, huskier than she remembered. "It's been a long time, Caroline."

The words would have sounded trite if there wasn't so much emotion lying just beneath the surface.

Caroline nodded. She knew she had to say something, anything, to break the almost unbearable tension between them.

"I didn't come to any of the other reunions. But twenty-five is . . . special."

"Yes."

She wanted to say, "I know you haven't come to them, either, so why are you at this one?" But she couldn't do that. Impossible as it was, she had to pretend that this unexpected meeting didn't affect her, that she hadn't spent twenty-five years avoiding him.

"May I have this dance?"

She intended to refuse. A dozen excuses were on the tip of her tongue. But before she could say a word, he simply pulled her onto the dance floor.

Above them, multicolored lights flickered and gay crepe paper streamers hung in giant loops. Caroline tried to focus on the decorations or on the dancing couples surrounding them. Anywhere but on Rafe.

Then he took her into his arms and they held each other for the first time in a long, long while. It was as if the years had dissolved and they were seventeen again. Back in the same gym where their hungry young bodies had once pressed tightly together, dancing to the same song.

Her head still came just to his shoulder, her cheek brushing the soft, smooth material of his dark jacket. Her breasts still lightly, and tantalizingly brushed his hard, flat abdomen.

As Rafe held her, his fingers lacing tightly with hers, Caroline was forcefully reminded of the heady physical sensations he'd once elicited in her.

She felt herself coming alive again in some primal way, like a half-dead flower thirsting for water, slowly blooming under a warm spring rain. All the passion she'd held back, even in her marriage, came flooding to the surface in a rush of desire and longing. Memories of hot summer nights spent learning about love under Rafe's tender, passionate tutelage relit a spark that had never really died.

But at the same time, she remembered what he'd done to her, and she hated him again, as strongly as she'd hated him at seventeen. The return of that hatred gave her the strength she needed to resist the powerful chemistry between them.

She stiffened in his arms, and she knew he sensed her withdrawal from him.

He watched her intently for a moment, then spoke in a deceptively matter-of-fact tone. "You've moved back to Clovis."

It was a statement, not a question, and Caroline wondered where he had heard. She'd only been back in town for a few days, and so far Marcia was the only one of her old friends she'd looked up. Surely, Marcia, who knew what had happened between them, would never have told Rafe.

At that moment she decided how she would handle it. They would make small talk like they would at any other alumni meeting. And when the dance was over, she would politely but firmly take her leave.

There was no way she could stay at the reunion any longer. All she wanted to do was get out of there, get home, go to bed and pull the covers over her head like a frightened child.

"You're not wearing a ring. I assume you're not married."

There was a barely veiled hint of hostility in the question that she didn't understand. He certainly had no right to be angry with her. She was the one who'd been hurt.

She responded in a barely civil tone that she hoped would discourage further personal questions. "No, I'm not married."

She didn't have to ask if he was. Marcia had already mentioned that he had never married.

"Divorced?"

The question was curt to the point of rudeness.

Forcing herself to look up at him, she answered with equal curtness, "Yes."

For an instant she caught a gleam of what was clearly satisfaction in his look. It caught her off guard and shook her tenuous self-control.

"So, Caroline, why did you come back?"

On the surface the question was innocent enough. Yet she felt somehow that there was nothing innocent about it. Her immediate impulse was to answer honestly, "To make a new start. To put the shattered pieces of my life back together again." But she couldn't say that, not to him. Instead, she gave part of the truth. "I decided I didn't want to live in the city any longer."

"The city? You mean, San Francisco?"

A sudden sharpness in his tone betrayed much more than mere interest. She had caught him by surprise, she realized. Of course, he hadn't known where she'd been living.

He repeated under his breath, "San Francisco..."

In spite of herself, she wondered why it seemed to strike him so forcefully. The two places were as different as a cosmopolitan city and a small, agriculturally oriented town could be. Still, they were actually only two hundred miles apart.

He said nothing further, and there was a long silence between them. It was worse than his questions, for it gave her mind nothing to concentrate on except his physical closeness.

To fill the silence, she asked, "What have you been doing all this time?"

The corners of his mouth curved in what might have been a smile, except that it was totally lacking in humor.

"I started a real estate development business. I'm doing all right."

She could tell by his tone, and by the obviously expensive Italian suit he wore, that it was an understatement.

She suspected he was extremely successful, and it didn't surprise her one bit. "Making it" had always mattered so greatly to him.

He asked casually, "Where are you living now?"

She briefly considered refusing to answer the question, but knew that was downright silly. She didn't want to let him see how he intimidated her.

"I'm back in my parents' old home. I inherited it when they died recently."

That would tell him a lot about her current situation, she knew. Being in the real estate business, he must be aware that her old neighborhood was no longer fashionable. It was, in fact, rather shabby. The fact that she lived there instead of in a nicer place would reveal her financial situation more clearly than she would have liked.

Looking up at him she had the odd sensation of reading his mind. He was thinking how ironic it was that now the gardener's son was rich and the banker's daughter was poor.

Yet she didn't feel at all bitter about it. Money had always mattered so much more to him than it had to her.

She waited for him to make the usual polite statement of sympathy regarding her parents' deaths. But he said nothing. His silence was worse than rude, she thought, it was insensitive, and that surprised her. Whatever had happened between them in the past, it didn't explain the hardness in his attitude toward her now.

Well, she could still be polite, even if he couldn't, she thought, then said out loud, "I'm glad you're doing so well, Rafe."

There was genuine sincerity in her voice, and she could see that it caught him off guard.

At that moment the song, which had begun to seem endless, finally was over. Immediately, the band began playing another, faster tune. But Caroline had no intention of remaining on the dance floor with Rafe.

Murmuring a barely audible, "Goodbye," she turned and threaded her way through the dancing couples.

She wasn't surprised when he followed her. Nevertheless, she jumped slightly when he took her arm and led her to a quiet corner.

"If you'll excuse me—" she began formally.

But he cut in, "You have all evening to talk to everyone else. And you and I still have so much catching up to do." Once more there was an underlying bitterness in his tone that puzzled her. But it didn't matter what was going on inside him. She simply couldn't keep up the pretense of a casual conversation any longer.

Seeing him again, feeling the touch of his strong hands, affected her more powerfully than she'd ever suspected it would. She didn't understand how it could still be that way after so many years apart. But it was. *Dear God,* she thought desperately, it was.

Before she could firmly take her leave of him, he went on, "What have you been doing with yourself all this time? Do you have any children?"

His expression was carefully neutral. His silver eyes betrayed no hint of real interest, and he hardly met her quick, startled look.

But she knew absolutely there was nothing casual about the question. Rage filled her. How dare he bring up that particular subject?

It was all she could do not to slap him. Instead she choked back the anger and the tears that threatened to spill out and turned to leave.

Grabbing her arm gently yet firmly, he stopped her.

"I want to see you again."

"No."

Pulling from his grasp, she continued walking quickly toward the door. He followed right behind.

"Why not?"

"We both know the answer to that. Leave me alone. Just leave me alone!"

The desperation in her voice must have gotten to him, for he stopped following her and simply stood watching as she fled from him.

Once outside the gym, her eyes became so blinded by tears that she didn't recognize the people around her. It was all she could do to make her way to her car. Rummaging clumsily in her purse, she finally found her keys and unlocked the door. She had to sit inside the car for a moment before she was collected enough to drive, then she made her way home with all the speed she could risk.

At home she made a pot of very hot tea, undressed and slipped on a turquoise silk caftan, a relic of her days as a well-to-do Hillsborough housewife. Then she curled up on her bed and poured a cup of tea with shaky hands. As she slowly sipped the soothing liquid, she finally let her mind go back to the time she tried so hard never to think about, the summer of 1961....

They were high school seniors. Caroline was the local banker's daughter. Rafael Marin came from the wrong side of the tracks, the half-caste son of a Mexican-American father who worked as a gardener, and an Anglo mother who was a waitress. One of Benito Marin's clients, in fact, was the Cummings.

Under normal circumstances, Rafe wouldn't have been part of Caroline's crowd. But he was a star athlete and darkly handsome, with a rakish charm that was at once dangerous and exciting to the privileged girls drawn to him. Even so, they had to date him on the sly because he wasn't welcome in their homes. After getting to know him, Caroline discovered how deeply he felt that humiliation.

She knew his string of seductions was a way of expressing that bitterness, and she was determined not to be just another of his conquests. It wasn't until the end of their senior year that she began to see the other side of him, the vulnerable side he had kept hidden. And once she saw that, she was lost to him.

By the middle of that hot, breathless summer following graduation, he had taken her from innocence to sexual knowledge. And she was bound even more strongly to him. When she gave him a book of Elizabeth Barrett Browning's poems and wrote on the flyleaf, "All my love forever," she meant it.

Then she discovered she was pregnant. Her parents were horrified, especially when she told them Rafe was the child's father and she wanted to marry him. Her father raved at her, then arranged an immediate transfer to another branch of his bank in Sacramento. He informed Caroline, who at seventeen was still underage and legally under his control, that she would never be allowed to see Rafe again. If she tried to do so, her father would have Rafe charged with statutory rape.

Though she knew she had to stay away from Rafe until her eighteenth birthday in December, she wanted desperately to communicate with him. And so, when his father came to do the yard for what was to be the last time, Caroline smuggled a note to him to give to Rafe.

The note said, "I have to go away, just until my birthday. Tell me you'll wait. Tell me you want me to come back to you."

Rafe never responded. As far as she knew, he made no attempt to get in touch with her, let alone to see her. And by the time she moved away from Clovis, two weeks later, she had come to the tearful conclusion that she had been just another of his conquests after all. He didn't want her and he wasn't about to take responsibility for their child.

Caroline's parents wanted her to give her baby up for adoption, preferably after being away for several months "visiting an aunt," so that no one would ever know. But she refused. For the first time in her young life, she stood up to them. She moved into a home for unwed mothers in San Francisco, and when her daughter came, she managed to support them both by working as a sales clerk in a department store.

Eventually, she married a very nice, very successful businessman, who was kind enough to legally adopt her daughter, Marina.

Thinking back about her marriage to Edward, Caroline faced a fact she'd always secretly known. She had never loved him. Not like she'd loved Rafe. That had been, at least subconsciously, Edward's main appeal for her. He could never hurt her as Rafe had done.

It was a brutal truth to face. But then, she thought with a sad half-smile, this was a night for facing brutal truths. Rafe had hurt her in the worst possible way a man could hurt a woman, and yet she was still drawn to him. There was no use trying to deceive herself about that.

She sighed deeply and took a long drink of the now tepid tea. Though San Joaquin Valley summers were scorching, and this was a typically hot July night, she suddenly felt very cold. Reaching down to the foot of the bed, she unfolded a faded blue and white striped afghan and wrapped it around her shoulders.

You'll be all right, Caroline Turner, she told herself with all the determination she'd mustered when she'd been eighteen and alone with a baby to care for. She had gone through tougher things than this, she reasoned, and survived. She would survive this unexpected meeting with the most haunting ghost from her past.

When she had decided to return to Clovis, she knew she might very well run into Rafe. It was too small a city for them to stay out of each other's way forever. She just hadn't expected to meet him so soon. And especially not in the very place where they had fallen in love.

She also hadn't expected him to have the same effect on her. Over the years, when she had allowed herself to think about him, she'd told herself his appeal would undoubtedly lessen as time went by. Young love was one thing, but they were both adults. She had changed inwardly, and she knew he must have too.

Except that he hadn't. At least not physically. He was the same male animal who could send her heart thumping with a glance, whose touch was electric. It didn't matter that she hated him. Her rational mind might feel that way, but her body wasn't behaving at all rationally.

She hadn't expected it to be like this. And she didn't know what she was going to do about it.

But as she set down her cup and reached over to turn out the bedside lamp, there was one thing of which she was certain. She must never give him the opportunity to hurt her again.

Rafe shifted down into fourth, then third, then second, and finally brought the sleek black Jaguar sedan to a halt at the side of the road that wound up through the foothills. Getting out, he angrily slammed the door, then walked to the edge of the precipice.

Below him, the San Joaquin Valley lay spread out in the dimness of the early evening light. Outside the city, the valley was a patchwork quilt of fields, orchards and vineyards, with gently sloping, barren brown foothills rising to the towering Sierra Nevada Mountains in the distance.

It was nearly nine o'clock. Soon the lavender-tinged twilight would dissolve and the few twinkling lights he could see would turn into hundreds of thousands. Clovis wasn't big, but Fresno, the city it bounded on the east, had a population of a quarter million.

And one of those people down there was Caroline.

The thought was sharp, painful, like the sudden thrust of a stiletto between his ribs.

Caroline.

She'd come back. She had walked back into his life after all this time, just when he'd convinced himself he had everything he could possibly want. He didn't need her, he'd told himself. He didn't want her.

Only that was a lie, damn it. The most stupid, most hopeless kind of lie because he was lying to himself.

His hands clenched into fists, and he wanted to hit something. But there was only dirt beneath his feet and air in front of him. No way to vent his rage, nothing to assuage his pain.

Why did she have to look the same? he wondered. The same golden hair falling straight to her shoulders. The same soft brown eyes with all the appealing vulnerability of a fawn. The same slender, long-legged body that had driven him into a frenzy of desire—the desire to possess her, to make her respond to him as fiercely as he responded to her.

And yet, he thought, she wasn't exactly the same. The vulnerability was there as before. But she was a woman now, not a girl. And all the more compellingly attractive because of that.

He wasn't a man given to second-guessing himself, but now he felt he'd made a mistake in going to the reunion.

He wouldn't have gone if it hadn't been for that conversation with his secretary. Trudi had casually mentioned that her best friend's mother, Marcia Bennett, was a classmate of his and was one of the organizers of the reunion. When she asked if Rafe was going, he said no, he never bothered with those boring affairs.

She agreed it would probably be deadly dull to see old classmates. Of course, Mrs. Bennett was excited about it because her best friend from high school, who'd just moved back into town, would be there.

Rafe had hesitated for a moment, telling himself he was being ridiculous. Marcia had been a popular girl at Clovis High, with lots of friends. But finally, almost against his will, he'd asked if the best friend's name was Caroline Cummings.

No, Caroline Turner, Trudi replied blithely.

He realized that Turner must be her married name. And so he had gone to the reunion, specifically to see Caroline. Well, he'd seen her. But it hadn't gone at all as he'd expected.

He had shown her he wasn't the same poor, half-caste boy she'd hurt so deeply. And when he'd sensed how different their financial situations were now, the irony was sweet.

Bittersweet, he admitted reluctantly. Because the truth was, as soon as he saw her he wanted her again. With all the old aching longing that no other woman had even begun to ignite in him.

God knew there had been enough women. When he was young and struggling, they were drawn to his potent sexual appeal. As he became more successful, they were drawn to his money and position as well. But not one had lasted for longer than a few months. And not one had breached the impenetrable wall around him.

He hadn't set out to break their hearts. He just hadn't cared when it happened.

A cool breeze came up to lightly caress his face and ruffle his hair, as the last of the twilight faded into darkness. But the breeze didn't cool the heat penetrating through to his very bones. Just remembering how Caroline had felt as he'd taken her in his arms, exactly as he had done countless times in the old days, was enough to make his pulse race and his breath quicken.

And that made it all so much worse. She had hurt him in a way that could never be forgiven, and yet he couldn't help wanting her. He was furious at his body's betrayal. But it did no good to rail against it. The feelings were there, whether he wanted them to be or not.

He knew he had to do something. Now that she was back, and they would certainly be running into each other, he couldn't simply ignore her and hope his feelings would go away. They hadn't gone away in twenty-five years.

No, he had to do something about them. Something that would once and for all cleanse his mind and heart of her. Something that would complete what was left undone from the past and settle the old score.

Gradually, an idea took shape in his mind and he knew what he would do. His firm, sensual mouth curved almost imperceptibly.

There was one heart he would set out to break.

Chapter Two

Caroline was still in bed when the phone rang early the next morning. She hadn't slept well the night before and stifled a yawn as she picked up the receiver. Only one person had her unlisted number, so she knew who it would be before she heard the familiar, cheerful voice.

"Hi, did I wake you?"

"No, Marcia. I was just lying here thinking about getting up. About last night..."

"It's okay, you don't have to explain. I looked all over for you, then I saw Rafe. I assume you two ran into each other."

"Yes. It...was rather traumatic."

"Oh, Carrie, I'm so sorry. I never dreamed he'd show up."

"I know. Don't worry, it wasn't your fault."

"Still, I can imagine how unpleasant it was for you."

There was real concern in her voice, but also an inescapable curiosity. Caroline knew Marcia wondered what exactly had happened. She couldn't blame her. But she wasn't up to talking about it.

Fortunately, Marcia was an old friend and Caroline could be frank with her.

"I'd rather just forget the whole thing, okay?"

There was a barely audible sigh of disappointment over the line. "Okay. I understand." However, she couldn't resist adding, "But he's still incredibly sexy, isn't he?"

"Marcia."

"Okay, okay. I know when to zip my lip. I'm sorry his showing up had to ruin the reunion for you. It was really fun."

"What happened?"

"Well, by the end of the evening there were some interesting pairing offs. Jack Hadley and Mary Lee Curtis were all hot and heavy on the dance floor again."

"Really? At graduation she told him she wouldn't have anything more to do with him if he was the last man on earth."

Marcia chuckled. "I remember. But she's had twenty-five years to cool down. And they're both divorced now, you know. By the way, you should have seen Krista Donovan ogling Danny Syms. I think you two went to the junior prom together, didn't you?"

"Yeah. I saw him with a gorgeous blonde on his arm. Who is she?"

"That's his brand new wife. He waited a long time to get married, and when he did he picked a winner. And he wasn't about to push her aside, even for Krista. It's ironic, isn't it? In high school she was the head cheerleader, the girl all the boys wanted. Danny couldn't get near her. Now, she's been divorced twice and wishes she'd paid more attention to him. He's a real successful attorney, you know.''

Krista becoming interested in the boy she'd once so blithely ignored wasn't the only irony from the reunion, Caroline thought soberly. Suddenly, she didn't want to rehash old times.

"Marcia, I've got to go. I still haven't finished unpacking, and I've got a million things to do today."

"Are you coming to the party at the Hilton tonight?"

"No. I . . . I don't think that would be a good idea."

"Oh, Carrie, are you sure? You'll miss a great time. Maybe he won't come tonight."

"I can't count on that. And I just can't face him again."

"Was it that bad?"

Caroline was thoughtful for a moment. Finally, she answered slowly, "We didn't exactly fight, or anything. It was just...so much more emotional than I'd expected it would be. I wasn't at all prepared for how I would react to him."

"You mean you were very angry at him?"

"No, not exactly." She hesitated, then sighed heavily. "Well, as you pointed out, he's still very attractive."

"You're interested in him?"

That was a mild description of the way her body had responded to his, she thought wryly.

"He still gets to me, I guess. And I don't intend to let that happen again. I've been down that road before, and it's marked Dead End."

"You wouldn't be the first couple to rekindle an old romance. Look at Jack and Mary Lee. By the way, Gary Bedrosian told me he wanted us to pick up where we left off in high school."

"Really? Are you going out with him?"

Marcia laughed. "No way. He wouldn't give me his home phone number, because he said his wife might answer!"

Caroline laughed along with Marcia. "Sounds like he hasn't changed a bit."

"No, unfortunately. But getting back to you and Rafe, how about it?"

"Forget it. There's too much history between us. We did more than share some heavy makeout sessions in the back seat of a '57 Chevy, remember?"

"I know. I'm sorry if it seemed like I was trying to make something out of it. I'm a romantic at heart. I can't help hoping for happy endings."

"Marcia, you're a widow and I'm divorced. So far, happy endings seem to have escaped both of us."

"So far. Neither of us is down for the count yet."

Caroline couldn't help smiling at Marcia's irrepressible optimism. She'd always been that way and, clearly, always would be.

"I've really got to go now, Marcia. Those boxes aren't going to unpack themselves."

"Okay. I wish you were going to be there tonight, but I do understand. How about lunch?"

"Not today, thanks. I'll be filthy from all the unpacking and cleaning, and I won't feel like taking time out to clean up."

"Not even for McDonald's?"

Caroline laughed softly. It was an old joke between them that it didn't matter how unkempt they looked when they went to McDonald's because they weren't likely to meet the men of their dreams there.

The man of her dreams . . . suddenly a picture of Rafe came into her mind. It was astonishingly vivid and very disturbing.

"Marcia, I've got to run. Talk to you tomorrow."

She hung up abruptly, before Marcia could inadvertently say anything else that would remind her of Rafe.

Showering quickly, she then dressed in faded jeans and a pink T-shirt and pulled her hair back with a matching pink headband. After eating a light breakfast of coffee and toast, she went right to work.

The movers had put all her furniture in place, but most of the boxes remained to be unpacked. The house itself, which had sat empty for several months following her parents' death in a boating accident, was quite dusty.

Before settling down to the hard work, she walked slowly through the house, remembering how it had once looked and deciding how she would redecorate it now. It was a typical post-World War II ranch style home, relatively small and unimposing, yet with a simple charm. There were shutters inside and out and hardwood floors. Off the small dining room were French doors leading to a tiny brick patio.

At one time, her mother had kept masses of brightly colored geraniums and daisies in clay planters on the patio. Caroline decided to do the same, as soon as possible. That would help dispel the air of abandonment that permeated the place.

Also, she decided, she would paint the inside a nice, cheerful, creamy yellow. And cut down the flowered chintz drapes she'd saved from her Hillsborough home to fit the smaller windows. Then, with some bright throw rugs on the floors, the place would be quite pleasant.

It would never be as opulent as her other home had been, she thought with a rueful smile. But it was hers. For now, that was enough.

The important thing was that she felt comfortable here. Until her family's sudden move when she became pregnant, theirs had been a happy home. Her parents were overprotective in many ways, but they did love her. And while they'd been angry and bewildered at her insistence on keeping her child, they had eventually accepted the situation.

Now, looking around her at the house that had sat empty and quiet for too long, Caroline decided it was time to make it a happy home again.

She set to work dusting, cleaning and unpacking. Stopping only for a quick sandwich at lunchtime, she worked on through the afternoon.

She was unpacking books, placing them in the built-in shelves on either side of the red brick fireplace, when she noticed one that Edward had given her years before on a trip to England. It was about English cottages, which Caroline adored. Sitting cross-legged on the floor, she thumbed through the book, enjoying once more the lovely, soft hued paintings of quaint cottages.

Gradually she stopped focusing on the cottages, and leaning back against the sofa, thought about her marriage. She had cared deeply for Edward. He was a good husband and father, and certainly a good provider. He'd given her everything most women dream of—a luxurious home, financial security and the freedom to devote herself to volunteer work and her hobby, making copies of antique porcelain dolls.

And most importantly he'd given Marina his name. Looking back on it now, Caroline realized that that was the main motivation in her marriage. She wanted her daughter to have a father, and she desperately wanted to erase the stigma of illegitimacy that Marina would have otherwise grown up with.

On the surface, her life with Edward was idyllic. She tried to be the perfect wife to him, to repay him for his love and generosity. She had thought they had a happy marriage, much happier than many she'd observed. She certainly never expected her life to change so drastically, to wind up at forty-two starting over again, alone, and nearly broke.

But with the wisdom of hindsight, she could see how it had happened. She understood why, when his business went under and he lost everything, he turned to another, younger woman to reassure him of his worth and desirability. Because no matter how deeply Caroline had cared for him, she had never really loved him.

But, like Scarlett O'Hara, she wasn't going to think of that. Now, she realized, she had to put her life back together again.

I will make a new life for myself, she thought with her characteristic quiet determination. *I will make this shabby old house a pleasant home. I will find a job. And somehow I will be all right.*

The ringing of the doorbell startled her. Looking up, she was surprised to see how late it was. The light had faded and it was time to turn on lamps.

As she walked to the door, brushing her dusty hands on her jeans, she assumed it would be Marcia, stopping by for a quick chat before going on to the party. She was glad of the unexpected company after being alone all day. But when she opened the door, she came face to face with Rafe.

He stood there nonchalantly holding a bottle of red wine with one hand and a box containing a pizza with the other. He was casually dressed in tan slacks and a short sleeved, V-necked white T-shirt. And he looked even more wonderful than he had the night before.

"I thought you might not be going to the party tonight. So I brought dinner."

He was absolutely casual, as if nothing had happened between them. Her nearly hysterical flight from him the night before might never have happened.

As his gray eyes took in her disheveled appearance, she was torn between anger at his cool presumption and embarrassment at being caught looking like she was.

Pulling herself together, she said, "I'm not dressed for guests. So if you'll please leave...."

He smiled in that slow, sensual way she remembered so well. The smile didn't light his eyes as it once had done, but it was still effective. Caroline felt her resolve weakening.

"Come on, Caroline. This is no Trojan horse. Just a pizza and a bottle of wine." He finished pointedly, "You look hungry."

Suddenly, she realized she was absolutely ravenous. She'd eaten very little all day and had worked almost nonstop. The pizza smelled delicious and the wine looked rich and inviting.

But, she reminded herself, she didn't want to have anything to do with this man. Certainly not in the intimacy of her own home.

"Rafe..."

"I'm sorry we got off on the wrong foot last night. I'd like to make amends."

The apology caught her completely off guard. It wasn't at all what she'd expected of a man whom she remembered as having a fierce pride. It was oddly touching. And, she discovered, well nigh irresistible.

Watching her hesitation, he coaxed, "Come on, Caroline. It's only a pizza."

Only a pizza. And the Hope diamond was just another rock.

She opened the door wider.

"Come in. You can put those on the table. I'll just go clean up a bit."

"Don't feel you have to change." His eyes narrowed appraisingly as he gave her a long look. "You do wonders for jeans and a T-shirt."

Meeting his look, she felt her breath catch in her throat. She started to speak, but found she couldn't. Without saying another word, she turned on her heel and hurried into her bedroom, closing the door firmly behind her.

When she emerged five minutes later, she had changed into the turquoise caftan she'd worn the night before and pulled her hair into a sleek knot at the nape of her neck. She'd washed her face and hands but hadn't bothered with makeup or jewelry. She didn't want Rafe to think she was trying in any way to impress him.

This was only a dinner, she told herself. And a very casual one at that. It didn't mean anything. And it certainly wasn't going to lead to anything.

He smiled again when she entered the dining room.

"That's a terrific color on you."

"Thank you."

She was polite but distant and intended to remain that way.

While Rafe poured wine into two glasses he'd gotten from the china hutch in the corner, Caroline went into the kitchen and returned with plates and napkins. Before she sat down, Rafe handed her a glass of rich burgundy wine.

Holding up his glass, he made a toast. "To the future."

When she looked wary, he went on, "I want to put the past behind us, Caroline. A long time has passed, a lot has happened to both of us. We were just kids before.

We're older now and, hopefully, wiser. I'd like to think we can be friends.''

Friends... it sounded odd, coming from the only man she'd ever loved. But he was right—they had just been kids when they'd known each other before. They weren't perfect, and they had made mistakes. They were young and scared when they went through their trauma. Whatever pain they'd caused each other was in the past. Perhaps it was time for forgiveness. To lay the past and all its unhappiness to rest.

But as soon as she thought that, she knew it would be hard, if not impossible. She could never forget what he'd done to her and to their child. She simply wasn't that magnanimous.

Her brown eyes met his gray ones and she said honestly, "I don't think you and I can be friends, Rafe. As they say, there's too much blood under the bridge."

His expression was thoughtful. "I understand. But we can try."

As far as she was concerned, it was certainly much safer, much easier, to simply stay out of his way. She asked bluntly, "Why should we try?"

As if reading her thoughts, he responded, "We're bound to run into each other. Clovis is pretty small, after all. I don't think either one of us wants to go on feeling awkward and angry around the other."

He was right, Caroline admitted reluctantly. They were bound to meet again, whether or not she wanted it to happen. It would be embarrassing, not to mention downright painful, to keep repeating the emotional upheaval of that scene at the reunion.

And besides, she told herself, it didn't mean they would be involved in any way. It would just mean that when they happened to run into each other, they would be civil.

She didn't really think they could be friends, but perhaps they could at least not be enemies.

At any rate, as Rafe said, they could try.

He was watching her patiently. As she recalled, patience wasn't one of his virtues, and she wondered what other unexpected qualities he had developed. Then she quickly decided she was wondering entirely too much about him.

Flashing him an irritated look, she said, "We don't have anything to offer each other."

"Don't we?"

His attitude was so close to smugness that she wanted to throw the wine in his face, which was totally unlike her. She realized angrily that all it took was five minutes in his presence, and she was reacting like a volatile teenager. While he, oddly enough, was cool as the proverbial cucumber.

Caroline fought to bring her anger under control, then eyed him thoughtfully. "You used to have quite a temper. Since when have you been so damn nice?"

He smiled dryly. "I realized pretty quickly that I wouldn't be successful in business by telling everyone to go to hell. I've learned to contain my emotions."

Have you? she thought. *And what of all that glorious passion? Is it contained, too?*

It was impossible, she realized, to have an objective conversation with him. She was too aware of him physically. The memory of the passion they'd shared was still all too intense.

If he were any other man . . . but he wasn't. He was the man who'd taken her from innocence to knowledge, who'd spoiled her for any other man. The man she couldn't get out of her system, despite the fact that he'd proven he was no damn good for her.

Setting down her glass of wine, she began, "This isn't going to work. I'm not comfortable around you."

"I realize it's awkward. We need to get to know each other again."

Getting to know him wasn't part of the bargain, she thought. "Rafe..."

At that moment, her stomach growled. For a split second, she was intensely embarrassed. Then they both broke into laughter together.

"I'm starving, too, Caroline," he said with a grin. "Let's eat."

He handed her a slice of pizza loaded with everything that could possibly go on it. She bit into it gratefully. Somehow, all that mattered now was eating. The worst of the awkwardness between them was over.

They ate in silence for a few minutes. The wine turned the casual meal into something special. It was very expensive and very good. As she swallowed it, Caroline felt its mellow warmth slide down her throat and permeate her entire being. For the first time since going to the reunion the night before, she began to relax slightly.

"Tell me about your business. You said you're in real estate development."

Rafe nodded. "Yes. It's mainly commercial office buildings, shopping centers, that sort of thing."

"How did you get into it?"

"I wanted to make a great deal of money fast," he answered frankly. "In the sixties and seventies, in California, the easiest way to do that was real estate."

"Money matters a lot to you."

"It matters a lot to everyone."

"Not everyone."

His gray eyes met her brown ones guardedly. "People stopped caring about my background after I made my first million."

He wasn't bragging about his income, she knew. He was simply stating a hard fact. She had no idea what to say that wouldn't sound naive or patronizing.

Before she could frame a response, he went on, "Nowadays, even your father would find me socially acceptable."

She flashed him a quick, curious look. Was that why he'd abandoned her? she wondered. Because he couldn't stand up to her father? Remembering his strength and rebelliousness, she found that impossible to believe.

She wanted to ask him, but that would mean venturing into dangerous territory. Forbidden territory. If they were to have even the most superficial relationship, they must never look back.

Finally, she said defensively, "My father wasn't a bad man, Rafe. He was a product of his time."

Again there was that half-smile that was so devoid of real amusement. "Let's change the subject, shall we? Tell me about your marriage."

She was completely caught off guard by the abrupt, personal question. Her response was curt.

"I told you. I'm divorced."

"I know. Were you married long?"

She felt extremely uncomfortable discussing her marriage with Rafe. But to declare the subject off-limits would only make it seem even more interesting, she knew. Perhaps it would be better to cover it as quickly and superficially as possible, then let it drop.

"We were married for over twenty years. The divorce was just final recently." She and Edward had actually been married for twenty-two years. But they'd lied about their anniversary, adding two years, so Marina wouldn't guess she wasn't Edward's daughter. But Caroline wasn't about to go into that with Rafe.

"What happened?"

"That's a very personal question."

"Yes."

"I don't care to answer it."

"Do you still love him?"

"Rafe!" She was really angry now, and it showed in the golden sparks lighting her tawny eyes, and the tight line of her full mouth.

To her amazement, he laughed deeply.

"What's so funny?"

"You didn't used to be so feisty, Caroline. I'm glad to see you can stand up for yourself now."

"I can, indeed. So you can stop the inquisition."

His expression softened. "I honestly didn't mean it to sound like an inquisition. I was just curious."

Of course he was. Just as she was curious about him.

"Well, it works both ways. Tell me, why didn't you ever marry?"

"Because I didn't want to."

"A confirmed bachelor?"

He nodded.

She couldn't resist teasing him. "You must be one of the most eligible bachelors in Clovis. Do you have to beat off women with a stick?"

"I don't beat them off."

No, he wouldn't, she thought. He would thoroughly enjoy them.

He pushed his plate aside and leaned back in the chair, slowly sipping his wine. Over the rim of the blue-tinged crystal goblet, he watched her, as if waiting for her to make some move.

She began to feel uneasy under that steady gaze.

"Why are you looking at me so intently?"

"I was just thinking how incredibly young you look without even a scrap of makeup. And how beautiful."

She was completely at a loss for an answer.

He went on slowly, "You were always pretty, of course, but now...there's a maturity that makes your beauty much more interesting."

She felt herself blushing and would have given anything not to do so. She wasn't sure if he intended it, but he was getting to her. Pure and simple.

To steady her nerves, she took another sip of wine. Too late she realized that more wine was the last thing she needed. The heady combination of wine and the mesmerizing look in his compelling silver-tinted eyes was far too potent. It sent her senses reeling and made her thoughts turn to the realization of just how long it had been since a man had held her...kissed her....

Looking at Rafe at that moment she seemed to see him with a sudden clarity. The thick, shiny black hair, one lock of which fell rakishly across his wide forehead. The long, aquiline nose that hinted at distant Spanish ancestors. The mouth that could best be described as eminently kissable.

At one time that mouth had softened with humor and warmth. Now it was hard, even when it smiled. And the smile that had once tugged at her heart never seemed to reach his eyes. His gray eyes had always been guarded, but there had been moments of real intimacy between him and Caroline when he'd lowered his guard, and she'd seen the hurt, vulnerable person inside.

What had happened to make him so bitter? she wondered. He had the financial success, the social acceptance that apparently meant everything to him. So why wasn't he happy?

"What's wrong, Rafe?"

It was a second before she realized she had inadvertently spoken aloud. She hadn't meant to and would have taken back the words if she could, for they were too personal. But it was too late to take them back. The question hung in the air between them for one timeless moment.

He was startled. For an instant, something very like anguish showed in his expression. It was the first crack in his seemingly total self-control. Then it disappeared so quickly that Caroline almost thought she'd imagined it.

"Nothing is wrong with me, Caroline. But judging from your circumstances, I'd say there's a lot wrong with your life."

It was a harsh comment, and it surprised her, for they had seemed to have been drawing closer to each other for a minute.

She answered angrily, "I'm not as successful as you, Rafe. Is that what you wanted to hear? You must really get a kick out of that."

"Stop it!"

The no-nonsense order stopped the tears that were dangerously near the surface and brought her up short.

He went on carefully, "I didn't mean to kick you when you're obviously down. But it would be stupid to try to keep up polite social conventions between us, wouldn't it?"

It would, indeed, she knew. They had too much of a shared history for either to pretend ignorance of the other's problems.

"Caroline, if you need a job, I can help."

It was a generous offer under the circumstances, one she would never have expected him to make. But it was one she couldn't even consider taking. She shook her head slowly. "No, thanks."

When he started to protest, she continued quickly, "I mean that, Rafe. Thank you for the offer. But I really couldn't accept. And besides, I'm not broke, you know. I'll have to go to work eventually, but I can afford to coast for a while."

"Do you mean that, or are you just being proud?"

She couldn't help smiling. "I mean it. Poverty didn't force me back into this house, you know."

"What did?"

The question was fraught with a deeper meaning that she couldn't quite grasp. But it was the answer that really bothered her. How could she explain that while she felt strong enough to start over, she was still scared enough to want to do it from a familiar base?

Finally, she answered carefully, "My parents never sold this house. They kept it as a rental. By the time I inherited it, it was paid for. Nowadays, with real estate prices being what they are, it seemed wise to move into it and fix it up."

"I see. It was a purely pragmatic decision."

It wasn't at all, and she could see that he didn't really believe it was. But he was willing to pretend that he believed so.

"Yes. And now, I hate to be rude, but I've been unpacking and cleaning all day, and I'm exhausted. Thank you for dinner, but would you mind—"

"Making an early night of it?" he finished for her. "Of course not. I understand."

They got up from the table together, and she walked to the door with him. As she opened it, she heard a cricket chirping somewhere in the darkness and felt the cool caress of a night breeze. The air was pungent with the strong, sweet scent of an ancient magnolia that shaded most of the front yard.

It was a classic summer night in the San Joaquin Valley, and Caroline realized that she had missed it desperately without even being aware that she did so.

As he stepped out onto the porch, Rafe turned to her. "I'll call you."

"Please don't. We've made a truce of sorts. I think that's enough."

"You're wrong. I'll call you."

Before she could argue, he turned and strode down the walkway toward his car parked at the front curb.

For a moment Caroline stood silhouetted in the light flooding through the doorway. Then she stepped back and closed and locked the door. But she didn't move back inside. Instead, she leaned against the door and wondered if she would have the courage to refuse him when he called.

Chapter Three

I can't believe what you've done with this place in only a week," Marcia said as she looked around admiringly. "It looks like a different house."

Sunlight streaming in through the curtainless windows bathed the cream-colored walls in a golden glow. The house was very bright, sunny and cheerful.

"I love the color you've painted in here."

"A teenage boy from down the street helped with the painting," Caroline responded. "He isn't a professional painter, but he did a pretty good job. His family are Hmongs, you know, the refugees from Vietnam. Very hardworking people."

Looking around, she sighed happily. "Everything's finished now, except for the drapes. I couldn't stand those ratty old ones, so I took them down, even though the ones from my old house aren't ready. I'm having the boy's mother, who's a professional seamstress, cut them down."

"Well, I'm amazed. I wouldn't even have finished unpacking this quickly, let alone redecorating."

Caroline grinned. "Well, I didn't have anything else to do."

She went into the kitchen and called back through the open door, "Do you want wine or iced tea?"

"Iced tea," Marcia replied. Walking over to a corner, she stood admiring a glass-fronted case that held a collection of copies of antique porcelain dolls that Caroline had made. "Carrie, these dolls are gorgeous!" she called out.

"Thanks. I'm rather proud of them," Caroline answered from the kitchen.

A moment later she came out carrying a tray with a pitcher of iced tea and two glasses. She set it on the dining room table, then walked over to the case where Marcia was still looking at the dolls.

"How do you make them?" Marcia asked.

"From molds. It's a complicated, time-consuming process. I have to sand and polish the porcelain several times to get it to the point where it has that waxy glow."

Opening up the case, Marcia picked up a blond doll with round blue eyes and commented, "Her eyes are so clear they reflect things."

"They're called paperweight eyes. They're made from hand blown lead crystal. That particular doll is called Pamela."

Marcia grinned. "You even gave her a name?"

"I didn't, the original designer did. All of the dolls I do are copies of dolls originally made in the 1800s."

Looking at the doll closely, Marcia exclaimed, "Even the fingers are separate, with little fingernails carved in them. How exquisite!"

"And time-consuming," Caroline said ruefully. "But it means a lot to me to do it right, the way it was originally done when doll makers took great pride in their craft. I actually carve the features in the porcelain to make the faces more expressive."

"I've seen dolls similar to these in department stores, but they're not nearly this nice. Why, this one must have half a dozen lace petticoats under her dress."

"I sew their clothes, too. It's really fun dressing them up in old-fashioned clothes."

"How much do the real antique dolls sell for?" Marcia asked curiously.

"Well, one sold recently for twenty-five thousand dollars."

"You're kidding! For a doll?"

Caroline nodded. "Good quality handmade reproductions like mine go for several hundred dollars."

"What made you decide to take this up as a hobby?"

Caroline shrugged. "I had time on my hands when Marina started school. At first I made them for her, then after a while it was something to fill my time while Edward spent all his time at the office. But enough of this. Lunch is ready, and I'm starved."

Reluctantly Marcia pulled herself away from the lovely dolls with their velvet and satin dresses and elaborate bonnets. While she sat down at the dining room table, Caroline went back into the kitchen and returned almost immediately with a casserole dish.

"Mmm, looks good, Carrie. What is it?"

"Shrimp casserole. There's strawberry mousse for dessert."

"Carrie, how do you do it all? Cook, decorate, make dolls..."

"You forget I had a long time as a housewife to perfect all those homely talents. Edward wanted a full-time wife, and I was happy to be one. Only now that I need to work, I'm finding that those skills aren't in high demand. I can do a fair job of decorating my own home on a limited budget, but I'm certainly not a professional decorator. And I can whip up a passable meal for a dozen last minute dinner guests, but I'm no chef."

"I know what you mean. When Carl died, I was fairly well-off financially, but I wanted to go back to work. Jill and Jason were teenagers, busy doing their own thing, and didn't want me devoting myself entirely to them. It got to be boring going shopping and having lunch with friends."

"How did you find your job?"

"Celia, my boss, is Carl's cousin. She was kind enough to let me go to work for her at her dress shop, even though she knew I had no experience at all. Gradually, I worked my way up to manager. Carrie, I wish you'd reconsider coming to work at the shop. I'm not just offering the job as a favor, you know. We really need another salesperson."

"I appreciate the offer. Really. But I had enough of that the two years I worked at Macy's."

Marcia smiled ruefully. "I know what you mean. There are days when it's all I can do not to tell some obnoxious customer exactly what I think of her. Actually, I'd like to get into something different now, something where I could be my own boss, but I have no idea what. I don't really have any contacts in any other field."

"I know what you mean about contacts. Unfortunately, you're the only person I kept in touch with in

Clovis. I don't have any contacts to approach for a job either."

Suddenly Caroline remembered Rafe's offer, but she didn't tell Marcia. She was still determined not to accept it.

"Do you ever sell your dolls? I'd love to buy one for my niece's birthday."

"I've sold several to acquaintances in San Francisco. And a boutique up there wanted to take some on consignment, but I didn't have the time to make them in a large enough quantity. I'd be happy to give one to you. Just pick out whichever one you like."

Marcia was uncharacteristically silent for a long moment. Finally, she looked intently at Caroline. "I have an idea."

Caroline's smile was warmly indulgent. "You always have ideas. As I recall your ideas have gotten both of us into trouble more than once."

But Marcia didn't return her smile. Instead, she said quite seriously, "Let's open up our own shop."

"But what would we sell?"

"Your dolls."

"Marcia, that's ridiculous."

"Why? You said yourself that a San Francisco boutique wanted them. If they're good enough for San Francisco, they're good enough for Clovis. There's nothing like that here now."

"Probably for a very good reason. Maybe there isn't any demand."

"Carrie, your dolls are exquisite. Much finer than any I've seen in department stores."

"That's because I make them entirely by hand. But it's a lot of work. Besides making the dolls themselves, I sew the clothes and search through secondhand stores for real old lace. When I do sell them I have to charge a great deal to make it financially worthwhile.''

"Money's no object.'' At Caroline's grimace, Marcia hurried on, ''I mean it. People are always willing to pay for quality. And these are so special. Heirlooms, really.''

"Are you serious?''

"I've never been more serious in my life. Oh, Carrie, I can see it now. Just a small boutique to start out. We want to keep our overhead down. Maybe we could call it The Dollhouse. You must have three dozen dolls already made in that case over there. That would be enough to start out.''

"But if you're right, and there's a demand for them, what would we do once we sold out? It takes me weeks to make one doll.''

"We'll get some help then. At any rate, we can worry about that when the time comes. Oh, Carrie, wouldn't it be fun?''

It would, indeed. But Caroline knew that successful businesses were rarely based on having fun.

"I can make the dolls. But I don't know anything about running a business.''

"I do. I run the dress shop single-handedly when the owner's away. I even help keep the books. Carrie, it would be a perfect arrangement—you're the creative half, I'm the business half. What a partnership!''

Caroline laughed happily. "You make it sound so easy. Like in all those 1940s' movies where a bunch of kids say, 'Let's put on a show in our backyard,' and the next thing you know they're on Broadway.''

The expression on Marcia's round face sobered. "I know it wouldn't be easy. Believe it or not, beneath this silly exterior beats the heart of an experienced business-woman. The dress shop nearly went under at one point, so I know how hard it can be to keep a small business afloat. But I really think this could work.''

"It would be a big risk."

"I know. I'm willing to take that risk. This is what I've been looking for. A chance to do something on my own."

"But do you really want to quit your job?"

"You bet! I don't need the money, and it's gotten so boring. I haven't quit before now because I didn't have anything better to do."

"This is so impulsive."

"Not really. The only financial investment we'd have to make would be on the lease of a shop. It would probably have to be for six months, at least. But if we can find a small place in one of the less expensive shopping centers, that wouldn't amount to a great deal. Our main investment would be our time."

"That's one thing I have in abundance," Caroline admitted slowly. After a moment, she went on, "I think my resources could stretch to six months. Although I might have to give up something optional, like eating, toward the end."

Marcia giggled. "Don't worry. We're going to be making a small fortune by then."

"Only a small one?"

They laughed together.

Marcia rose from the table. "Let's skip the strawberry mousse, which my thighs don't need, and go to a commercial realtor."

"Right now?"

"Yup. It may take awhile to find just the right shop. Location is crucial, you know."

"Maybe we should take some time to think this over."

"Carrie, if ever there was a time when both of us needed to stop being safe and try something new it's right now. I don't want to spend the rest of my life in that dress shop. And I'll bet you're too creative to spend yours in an office."

Caroline realized the truth of Marcia's words. She had thought a great deal about what kind of job she could get with her limited work experience and lack of a college education. She knew she'd probably have to settle for the most menial sort of office job, at least in the beginning. And, as Marcia said, she wouldn't be happy doing that.

Looking up at Marcia's excited, hopeful expression she reached a decision. "Okay. But I suspect we're both crazy."

"Crazy like a fox," Marcia replied.

Caroline returned home alone late that evening. She and Marcia looked at a dozen small shops, none of which was quite right. It had been a particularly hot, sultry day, with a temperature that at one point was over a hundred. After driving around for hours, constantly getting in and out of the car in the heat, Caroline felt absolutely exhausted. Her beige linen blouse clung to her shoulder blades, and her hair hung limply on her shoulders.

Heading straight to the bathroom, she stripped off her sweaty clothes, turned on the water in the tub and stepped in. Then she leaned back, closed her eyes tiredly and waited for the tub to fill.

So much seemed to have happened in so short a time. Her mind was reeling. She could hardly believe she and Marcia had committed themselves to such a risky venture. They had discussed it for all of ten minutes, then jumped right in. Yet she didn't feel frightened; she felt exhilarated.

There were any number of safer careers to pursue, she knew, but she wasn't in a mood to play it safe. During her marriage, she had done everything she could to help Edward achieve his dream of a successful business, and for quite a while he had achieved it. Now she wanted to have a dream of her own. And to make it come true.

The water was nearly to the rim of the tub. She turned off the faucet, then leaned back and let her body relax completely in the hot water that she'd lightly scented with jasmine bath salts. Idly, she swirled her fingertips on the surface of the water. For the first time in a long while she felt truly happy. And relaxed ... so relaxed ...

The ringing of the telephone woke her just as she was about to slip under the water. Shaking herself wide-awake, she stepped out of the tub, quickly slipped on her white terry cloth robe and ran to the phone on her bedside table.

"Hello?" Her voice was breathless.

"Caroline, it's Rafe."

Of course it was. The moment he spoke her name, she recognized his deep, resonant voice.

Something tightened deep in her stomach, and her fingers gripped the receiver a little more firmly. She felt a momentary embarrassment, and she pulled her robe closed as if he were there and could see her.

"Rafe ... how are you?"

He had told her he would call, yet somehow she was totally unprepared to hear from him. She was never at her best when caught off guard, and she cursed the nervousness apparent in the catch in her voice.

"I'm fine. And you?"

"Oh, just fine." Fervently she wished she didn't sound like such an absolute ninny.

"I called earlier, but you were out."

"Yes, Marcia and I were doing something."

"I only mentioned that because I didn't want you to think I would be rude enough to wait until seven o'clock to ask you out to dinner."

"You mean tonight?"

"Yes, unless, of course, you're busy."

She wasn't busy at all. And she wasn't sure there was anything to eat in her meagerly stocked kitchen. But in the week since she'd last seen him, she had told herself that if he did call, she would refuse him, point-blank. Somehow, she found that harder to do than she'd imagined it would be.

"Actually, I'm very tired...."

"Then you certainly don't feel like cooking. I thought we'd drive up to Pheasant Run. It's new since your time here and rather nice. It's up in the foothills, just past Oakhurst, and there's still enough light left to make it an enjoyable drive."

Caroline remembered what a nice drive it was, especially on a summer evening. But it would mean sitting in the close confines of Rafe's car, just the two of them, for forty-five minutes up there, and forty-five minutes back. Considering how he'd affected her the last time they were together, each minute would seem exquisitely long.

But how could she refuse politely? She was absolutely no good at lying, so making up an excuse was out. Besides, he wouldn't believe it. And she couldn't tell him the truth—that being with him disturbed her in a way she hadn't been disturbed since she was seventeen.

When her silence dragged out, he went on easily, "Come on Caroline. What do you have to lose?"

Only my heart.

When she still didn't speak, he coaxed in a lower, huskier tone, "I won't so much as touch you, if that's what you're concerned about. I promise."

She had an idiotic impulse to ask, "Cross your heart and hope to die?" but restrained herself.

She was being overly defensive, she decided. They had had dinner together once, and nothing had happened. There was no good reason why they couldn't do it again. Besides, she would thoroughly enjoy having a nice dinner that she didn't have to cook.

And she would enjoy seeing Rafe, an inner voice added wickedly. She gave up the fight. "All right. I can be ready in half an hour."

"Great. See you then."

As Caroline hung up, she had a fleeting sensation that she had just crossed some personal Rubicon. She told herself that was ridiculous. She was well armed against Rafe's charms, and besides, he'd promised to keep it platonic. So far, he hadn't made a move toward her, and there was no reason to suppose he would. Turning to her closet, she tried to decide what to wear.

An hour later they sat in Rafe's car. As he skillfully maneuvered the powerful car up the twisting mountain road, leaving the valley and the lower foothills behind them, he smiled inwardly. Caroline was sitting as far as possible from him, practically hugging the door. Her nervousness would have been quite funny if it wasn't so touching somehow.

Immediately, he steeled himself not to think in those terms. He didn't want to feel sorry for her. He didn't want her to get to him in any way. That wasn't part of the plan. The plan was for him to get to her. And then walk out on her as she had walked out on him.

Whenever he felt his resolve weakening, all he had to do was remember what had happened that summer they were both seventeen...what his father had said to him...what her father had told him....

Remembering, he felt the familiar sharp stab of bitter loss and humiliation. That bitterness had driven him to become financially successful, because if there was one thing people respected, it was money. Even if the person who made it was half-Latino.

It was ironic, he thought, how sought after he was now that he was one of the movers and shakers in town. Ironic and, somehow, not as satisfying as he'd expected.

Well, Caroline certainly wasn't going after him. She resisted him every step of the way. That was why he'd waited a whole week before calling her. He didn't want to come on too strong, because he knew without a doubt that wouldn't work.

She had been soft and pliant at seventeen, unable and unwilling to put up the slightest defense against his determined seduction. A memory flashed through his mind. He and Caroline were lying together on the soft, sweet scented grass of a mountain meadow, her body yielding to his, at first tentatively, then with growing passion.

Oh, yes, he thought, she'd been easy. But now she was different. Stronger. Nobody's fool.

Rafe glanced at her out of the corner of his eye. She looked smashing in a white gauze dress, cinched tight at the waist with a hot-pink sash. Open-toed pink sandals showed off her slender feet, and her only jewelry was a pink coral necklace. She'd pulled her hair up off her neck in a smooth chignon secured by an ivory comb. He preferred her hair down, flowing loosely to her shoulders. But he had to admit it looked very stylish this way.

Everything about her reflected the flair that San Francisco women seemed to have so effortlessly. There was nothing about her now of the shy, rather gauche seventeen-year-old who'd dressed conservatively, according to her mother's dictates.

Her figure was still the same, though. All long legs, barely rounded hips and high, firm breasts. Even after all this time, he remembered what she'd looked like, lying naked beneath him, the almost translucent quality of her skin and its incredible softness. Her creamy skin had looked so pale against his, and so fragile.

He had been nearly insane with wanting her. It had taken all his strength to hold himself back, to go slowly with her at first. Gentleness had been difficult, but crucial, because even at seventeen he had wanted to achieve more than his own satisfaction—he'd wanted hers as well.

He'd gotten it. Caroline had made him feel as no other woman had done before or since. And Rafe knew that he'd taken her to ecstasy and beyond. Slowly, inexorably, passion began to grow deep within him. Before this summer was over, he swore, she would lie naked beneath him again. It was only a matter of time.

"Is that the restaurant up ahead?" Caroline asked, breaking the silence.

Rafe nodded. "We're right on time."

In a moment he pulled the sleek Jaguar into the large parking lot of the Pheasant Run Restaurant.

"I didn't realize it would be so elegant," Caroline commented in surprise as she looked at the French Normandy architecture. "Somehow, I expected something a bit more rustic."

"The valley's gotten more sophisticated than it used to be. It's time we had a really good French restaurant."

Rafe got out of the car, then walked around to open Caroline's door. There wasn't a great deal of room between his car and the one parked next to it, so as he extended his hand to help Caroline alight, she was only inches from him.

For one long moment that seemed frozen in time, she stood facing him, her hand still in his. Her face was tilted up toward him, her golden eyes staring into his. There was a startled expression on her face, as if something had caught her unaware, and her full lips were parted slightly, invitingly.

The scent of her perfume was subtle yet seductive in the fresh mountain air. And the deep, scooped neckline of her dress had fallen over to one side, revealing a tantalizing glimpse of smooth, gently sloping shoulder.

Without thinking, he made an involuntary movement toward her, then checked himself just in time. It would have been so easy to cup her face in his hands and kiss her deeply. It was what he wanted badly. But this wasn't the time or the place, he knew. When he did kiss her, he intended to be completely in charge of the situation, not caught up in desire for her.

As he stepped back and let go of her hand, he saw a fleeting expression of disappointment cross her face. But almost immediately she had herself under control, and her expression revealed nothing of her turbulent thoughts. As they walked up the broad, red brick steps to the foyer, neither spoke.

Inside, the maître d' greeted Rafe warmly. "Monsieur Marin, how very nice to see you again. You are keeping well, I trust?"

"Quite well, thank you, Auguste."

"I have a lovely table for you, monsieur, right this way, please."

He led them to a small table for two next to a large window overlooking a brightly lit brick patio. As Caroline sat down, she looked around at the quaint country

French decor. Slate-blue paisley tablecloths, white faience rabbits and geese wearing colorful bandannas and prints of Impressionist paintings combined to create a warm and pleasant ambience. Tiny bouquets of fresh mountain wildflowers were the crowning glory.

Taking it all in, Caroline said, "This is really lovely."

"Thank you, mademoiselle. This is your first time with us?"

She nodded, and he went on, "And hopefully not your last. It improves the atmosphere of our little estaminet to have a lady who is so *très jolie*."

Caroline flashed a delighted grin at Rafe that clearly said, "He's a bit much, but it's rather fun getting such extravagant compliments."

Rafe wondered why Auguste had never been so taken with the other women he'd brought here. The answer, he suspected, was obvious—none of them had Caroline's unself-conscious class.

As Auguste handed Caroline a menu, he continued, "It is too bad that it has grown dark. There is a fabulous view from here. You must come for lunch sometime and enjoy it."

Rafe looked intently at Caroline and, without looking up at Auguste, responded, "I'll see to it she comes back."

Caroline's eyes met Rafe's and were held for one long moment before finally giving way and looking down demurely, ostensibly at the menu.

They had a bottle of deliciously bubbly champagne to start, then a crisp salad of fresh endive, *coquilles St. Jacques* accompanied by a dry white wine, and finally, for dessert, creme puffs shaped like swans. Although at first Caroline was reticent, gradually Rafe, aided by the effects of the champagne and the wine, drew her out. By the end of the meal she was telling him all about the proposed venture with Marcia.

"You probably think it's crazy," she finished, with a half-embarrassed smile.

Actually, he couldn't help admiring her talent and determination. It seemed odd to hear the woman he still thought of in a way as a shy, fragile teenager talking knowledgeably about making and selling antique dolls. For the first time it really struck him that Caroline was a mature, experienced woman, one with facets to her character he'd never even suspected.

He answered her frankly. "Not at all. You and Marcia have the two important ingredients—something worthwhile to sell and business experience. The only drawback I see is that there isn't unlimited growth potential."

"Oh, I don't care about that. I'm not trying to found an empire here. I just want to earn a fairly decent living doing what I enjoy."

"A modest goal."

She flashed him a wry look. "Not all of us are driven to be tycoons."

He smiled, genuinely amused. "Is that what I act like? A tycoon?"

"Of course. You drive a Jag, wear conservative but expensive clothes and are on a first name basis with maître d's."

She was teasing him and he was enjoying it.

"The only maître d' I'm on a first name basis with is Auguste."

"Ah, but he's French, and it's the French maître d's that really count."

"Is it?"

"It is, indeed. And you must admit I'm right about your clothes."

"Actually, I leave my wardrobe entirely up to my tailor. I'll have to ask him if he's been purposefully cultivating a tycoon image for me without my realizing it."

"And the car?" Caroline went on, clearly enjoying their banter. "Was that someone else's choice?"

"It's the best quality for the price."

"Do you always demand full value for your money?"

He looked at her intently. "Always. When I first began my business, a lot of high-powered people who were part of the establishment in this town assumed they could take advantage of me because I was just a dumb half-breed without a college education. They soon learned otherwise."

"You didn't go to college?"

He shook his head. "I preferred to get my education in the real world. What about you?"

"I didn't go either." She said nothing further, and Rafe sensed that she didn't want to pursue this subject. He knew why, too. College usually comes right after high school. But Caroline was busy having a baby after high school. His baby.

Where was that child now? he wondered, as he'd done so many times before. The agony of not knowing had never stopped eating away at him. The knowledge that somewhere out there he had a son or daughter he didn't know, was bitter indeed.

Abruptly all the anger he had felt toward Caroline through the years came flooding back. The fact that it was mixed with desire and a reluctant admiration only made it worse.

Gesturing toward the waiter, he curtly asked for the check. While waiting for it, he concentrated on finishing the last of his after dinner coffee and didn't speak to Caroline.

She sat opposite him, looking surprised and confused by the sudden chill between them. When they left, both were as quiet as they'd been when they'd arrived two hours earlier.

The entire trip back down the mountains was made in a strained silence. Rafe grew angrier by the minute, while Caroline looked more and more unhappy. It was a moonless night, far too dark to see any of the scenery they were passing, but Caroline kept her head turned toward the window anyway. Rafe kept his eyes on the road.

When he finally pulled to a halt in her driveway, she murmured a quiet, "Thank you for dinner," then started to open her door.

"I'll get that," he said curtly.

This time as he held open her door, he stood well away from her and she made a point of not getting any closer to him than she had to. As they walked together to her front door, neither touching nor speaking, Rafe felt the tension between them building.

Though he was still filled with an explosive anger, he couldn't help being aware of her physically, the way her full skirt swirled around her knees, the way her pale skin shone in the dim starlight, the way her breasts rose and fell beneath the thin gauze material of her dress.

And most of all he was aware of her soft, full mouth, the lower lip trembling slightly in her nervousness. He wanted to tease it gently with his teeth before crushing her lips beneath his possessively, as he'd once done in another time, another place ... another lifetime.

She took a key from her white leather clutch and opened the front door. Then, turning reluctantly toward

Rafe, she repeated, as if she could think of nothing else to say, "Thank you for dinner."

Before she could turn and walk through the door, he moved. With one long stride he was standing in front of her, their bodies nearly touching. She opened her mouth to protest, but no words came.

Reaching out, he gently pulled the ivory comb from her chignon, sending her honey-colored hair tumbling to her shoulders in charming disarray. Then one strong hand slid around her back, pulling her against him, while his other hand cupped her face.

"You said you wouldn't touch me!" she whispered breathlessly.

His voice was rough and completely unapologetic. "I lied."

Chapter Four

He didn't kiss her immediately. Instead, his lips lightly brushed her forehead, her eyelids, her cheeks, down her long, slender throat to pause at the pulse beating madly in the tiny hollow there.

Deep within her something long dead slowly came to life again. After the initial automatic resistance, she gave herself up to the exquisitely sensual pleasure of his touch.

Rafe's lips were sweet, Caroline thought helplessly, so sweet she could hardly bear it. Her arms hung limply at her sides. She couldn't have willed them to push him away if she tried.

Instead, she stood there, awash with happiness. And when his lips finally claimed hers, she opened up to him completely. Her surrender was so sudden she didn't even have time to wonder at it. She only knew that she wanted him, that her body was starved for his touch.

What a fool she'd been to tell herself this wouldn't happen, she thought dreamily. It was inevitable. And it was exactly what she wanted, though she'd refused to acknowledge it until this moment.

Her mouth opened eagerly to admit his warm, velvety tongue, and her lips returned his fierce passion. His hunger for her was intense, like a starving man suddenly faced with a banquet. It would have frightened her, had hers not been as intense.

Her hands went to his chest, her fingers gripping the open-necked white shirt beneath his tan gabardine blazer. Unconsciously, she moved toward him, her body pressing against his. Feeling the long length of him from his broad chest to his hard thighs stirred her blood and made her shiver. She felt at once white-hot and ice-cold. She felt wonderful.

When his lips finally left hers and moved once more to her throat, she murmured his name over and over again. *"Rafael, Rafael."* Its musical cadence flowed effortlessly off her tongue.

But as soon as she spoke, some spell seemed to be broken. He pulled back, as if suddenly brought to his senses. Startled by his abrupt withdrawal, she looked up into his eyes. What she saw there made no sense to her. There was the passion she'd just been forcibly reminded of, but there was also pain. Heart-wrenching pain. And an almost terrifying anger. Whether it was directed at her or himself, she couldn't tell.

Gripping her arms so hard that it hurt, he pushed her from him. And without saying a word, he turned and strode away.

Pulling herself together, she hurried inside the house. As she slammed shut the door, she heard his car start up and almost immediately roar off.

Feeling slightly disoriented, she walked through the dark house to her bedroom, where she switched on the pale bedside lamp. After undressing and slipping on a thin cotton gown, she crawled into bed and pulled the peach-colored satin coverlet up to her chin.

What happened? she wondered, fighting back tears. She could understand her weakness in giving way to his powerful sexuality even though she'd sworn to do no such thing. But she couldn't understand his reaction.

The logical explanation—that he'd stopped because he'd promised not to touch her—didn't wash. Rafael Marin was many things, but he was no gentleman.

She knew there was a moment when he had been as carried away as she was. And then he'd simply taken hold of himself and gotten away, leaving her feeling tortured by unsatisfied longing.

She didn't understand his behavior. Or the anger she'd seen in his silver-gray eyes. And most puzzling of all, she didn't understand the trace of fear that had been part of the anger.

Rafe nearly drove past his own house before realizing where he was. Applying the brakes, he slowed with a screech and made an abrupt turn into his driveway.

The long road wound up a low hill to a starkly modern house sitting alone on top of the hill. The 360-degree view of the valley was magnificent. Rafe had told himself that he chose this building site for the view. The fact that he was now, symbolically and literally, looking down on the town that had once looked down on him, was something he preferred not to think about.

He was more honest with himself regarding the aggressively modern design for the house itself. He wanted nothing to do with the past, even in architecture. But as he put his car away in the garage, then stormed inside, he faced the fact that the past had finally caught up to him with a vengeance.

In the huge living room, with its cream-colored leather furniture, he walked over to the floor to ceiling window and stared out into the night. In the distance below were the myriad twinkling lights of Fresno and Clovis. Overhead the sky was inky-black. In the silence and emptiness of the big house was an acute aura of loneliness that Rafe had never felt before.

And it was all because of Caroline.

Clenching his hands into tight fists, he thrust them into the pockets of his slacks. He was furious. With Caroline, but even more with himself. He had taken her into his arms with the intention of proving to her that he was still master of her body, that she was his for the taking if he wanted her.

Instead, the moment he had touched her, and especially once he'd felt her sweet surrender, he was lost to her. Holding her felt like coming home again after a long, long journey. All he had wanted to do was to bury his face in her silken hair, to feel her skin against his, to warm himself in that special glow that was hers alone.

Instead of dominating her, he had been in danger of being dominated by his need for her. That was something he couldn't allow. And so he'd forced himself to cut and run.

But one thing he had learned that night was that her resistance to him was paper-thin. She wanted him every bit as much as he wanted her. Things hadn't gone the way he'd planned this time, but next time would be different. Next time, he wouldn't let his emotions get in the way. He would be in complete control of the situation.

Next time . . .

Early the next morning, Rafe was on a tennis court at the club he belonged to, playing against his business partner. Though it was barely nine o'clock, already it was apparent that it was going to be a 100-plus day. Rafe's white tennis shirt clung wetly to his chest and back, and his white shorts outlined his firm buttocks.

Jim Hansen's blond hair hung damply down his forehead, and his fair skin glistened with sweat. He and Rafe were opposites in every way, not just physically and emotionally, but in terms of background. Jim was an architect who came from a long line of upper middle-class professionals. He had worked hard for his success, but he hadn't clawed his way to the top as Rafe had done.

They had met ten years earlier when Rafe had just left the real estate firm he'd been with and was starting his own company. He had needed an architect to provide the creative balance to his own business skill. Jim wanted the freedom to do his own thing, rather than remain in the secure but stifling atmosphere of his uncle's architectural firm.

To the amazement of everyone who knew the volatile, tough Rafe and the quiet, easygoing Jim, they meshed well. There was something in each that the other responded to on an elemental level. Without talking about it at all, they had gradually grown very close personally. At the same time their business became the most successful commercial development firm in Clovis.

Now, Jim stood behind the baseline, preparing to serve.

"Forty-love," he shouted.

As his left hand tossed the ball, his right went back, down, then up again in a smooth, powerful arc.

"Ace!" he shouted, whooping ecstatically, as the ball went past Rafe in a blur. "Game, set and match," he finished, his face split by a huge grin.

As the two men walked to the bench at the side of the court and picked up their things, Rafe said, "You owe me lunch after that massacre."

"Hey, I'll buy champagne if you want it. It feels so good to finally beat you. I knew I was making a fatal mistake when I taught you to play. This is the first time I've won a match in months."

Up on the clubhouse veranda, they ordered club sandwiches for lunch from the snackbar, then sat down at a patio table.

"Okay, what's wrong, Rafe?"

The question was an eery echo of Caroline's one earlier. It shook Rafe for an instant before he realized that Jim knew nothing about Caroline.

When Rafe didn't answer, Jim went on in his low-key way, "You weren't your usual self out there. Usually you're out for blood, but this time you were preoccupied about something. Are we going bankrupt and I just don't know it yet?"

Rafe met Jim's teasing smile. "No, it isn't business."

"Good. Ginny's got her heart set on a bigger house by this time next year. We're about to run out of room."

"Hey, you mean she's expecting again?"

"Again is the operative word, all right. Do you realize you'll be an honorary uncle for the fourth time?"

Rafe grinned happily. "That's really great. Congratulations."

"Can we drop the boys off at your house when she goes to the hospital?"

"Of course. I'll stock up on junk food. Last time Brian and Andy thought they were going to starve when they discovered I don't keep Twinkies and Pudding Pops."

"Thanks. I appreciate it. Well, keep your fingers crossed for a girl this time. Ginny really wants a daughter to dress up in all those frilly clothes and spoil even more than she's spoiled the boys. If we don't get a girl soon, I'll have my own baseball team one of these days."

"Whatever the little rascal turns out to be, you know you'll both be crazy about it."

"Yeah, I guess so. But it would be nice to have a daughter. The boys and I are very close, but there's just something about a little girl that's real special to a father."

Rafe felt a poignant pull at his heart. Whenever he thought of his own child, he always envisioned it as a daughter, for some reason. It made no sense, but the feeling was very strong.

Jim gave him a long, concerned look. "Rafe, what is it? Obviously, there's something on your mind."

As close as he felt to Jim, he didn't know how to tell him about Caroline. Finally, he replied awkwardly, "I'm dating someone new."

Enlightenment shone in Jim's pale-blue eyes. "Ah, so that's it. I should have known if it wasn't business, it had to be a woman."

Rafe stopped him. "Before you can start in with the questions, I'm going to pick up our sandwiches. I'll be right back."

When he returned with the food, Jim began easily, "Now, you know Ginny's gonna want to know all the details. Who is she, is she good enough for you, is she attractive?"

"She's Caroline Turner, she's very attractive and Ginny herself told me once that no woman was good enough for me."

Jim grinned. "That was the day you told her she was the best thing that ever happened to me, and you'd make sure I never forgot it. That was the same day you fired that cute secretary I was beginning to pay too much attention to."

"You were about to make a fool of yourself, and you know it," Rafe responded good-naturedly.

Jim sighed. "You're right. So how did you meet Caroline?"

"She's . . . an old classmate."

"From Clovis High?"

Rafe nodded.

"So you went to your reunion after all?"

"Yeah. I heard she moved back to town and I decided to renew our friendship."

"Considering how preoccupied you've been, I'd say it's more than a friendship."

"Could be," Rafe answered noncommittally as he bit into his sandwich.

"What's she do for a living?"

"She and a friend are starting a small business. They're going to sell porcelain dolls that Caroline makes."

"Mmm, sounds interesting. She and Ginny have something in common, then. You know Ginny still has every doll she ever got as a kid? She says she's saving them for her daughter."

"Apparently the dolls Caroline makes are copies of antique ones. Very expensive."

"Say, if they don't already have a shop maybe we could help them. There are one or two empty places that might be just the right size in our Valley Oak Center."

"I think Caroline would rather do this on her own. She hasn't shown any interest in my advice."

"The independent type, huh? She sounds more and more interesting. Don't tell me you've finally met your match."

"Very funny."

"Seriously, why don't you bring her over to dinner this weekend? Ginny will be dying of curiosity about her."

"Thanks, but I think I'll wait for a while. We've only just started dating."

"I see. You want to wait until you're sure about how it's going to work out."

Rafe was absolutely sure how it was going to work out. But he didn't say so to Jim.

Caroline surveyed the small shop in a shopping center in the affluent northwest area of Fresno. The L-shaped center faced two of the main streets in the area, so the location was excellent.

"What do you think?" Marcia asked in a whisper, as the Realtor who'd shown them the place made a point of walking to the far end of the room, leaving them to talk privately.

"It's perfect. But it's expensive."

"Yeah, but they're only asking for a three month lease. This is the last empty space in the center and they're anxious to fill it."

"What's really nice is that it would need so little done to decorate it. Just some nice wallpaper and the right shelves and doll cases."

"Oh, Carrie, let's take it!"

Caroline hesitated, torn between fear and excitement. But they'd looked at so many shops and this was the first one that really felt right. The location was great, and the short lease would be a godsend if the business failed.

She made a decision. "As the saying goes, 'no guts, no glory.' Let's do it!"

A half hour later they'd signed the lease and committed most of their cash assets to it. As they walked out of the realtor's office with two sets of keys to the shop, Caroline said, "We'd better open as soon as possible. We don't want to waste one day of our lease. Do you think we can have the place ready to open in a week?"

Marcia grinned. "We'd better. It was nice of the realtor to tell us about the place that's going out of business and selling its fixtures. Maybe we can pick up the shelves and cases we need there, at a reasonable price."

"Let's go over right now and see what they've got."

"Right."

By the end of the afternoon they'd purchased most of the furnishings they needed, including an ancient cash register, at far below their usual cost.

"Well, it's not computerized, but it'll do for the time being," Marcia commented, as she and Caroline loaded the cash register into the trailer they'd rented. "I'll get the kids to help us unload all of this first thing in the morning."

She and Caroline got into the car, and Marcia headed toward her house.

"After that we can pick up some wallpaper. It shouldn't take more than a few hours to get that done."

"Carrie, I have a confession to make. I've never wallpapered anything in my life."

Caroline smiled reassuringly. "Not to worry. I have. I learned how, out of necessity at first. That tiny little hole in the wall that was my first apartment in San Francisco was unlivable until I covered all the walls in big navy-blue and white stripes. It wasn't until we bought the Hillsborough house that I actually hired a paper hanger to do it for me.'' Marcia gave Caroline a curious look. Finally, she asked gently, ''Do you miss it? That whole lifestyle, I mean.''

Caroline's expression was thoughtful as she took a moment to frame her response. When she did speak, there was a new note of confidence in her voice.

''When I learned that we were going to lose everything, I was terrified. My first thought was about Marina, of course. I was glad that she was out of college and doing well on her own, so that it didn't really affect her. But I was scared for myself.''

''That's understandable. It had been over twenty years since you'd had to work as anything but a housewife.''

Caroline nodded. ''Exactly. I felt absolute panic. Which is why I came back here. I couldn't afford to live in the city any longer. But even if I could have, I still would have returned to Clovis. Because deep inside, I wanted to come home where I felt safe somehow. To lick my wounds and start all over again.''

''This is very different from what you were used to.''

''Yes. But you know what? I don't miss that life at all now. With Edward, I was living in a cocoon—safe, pampered, yet missing something vital.''

''What?''

''I'm not sure how to put it into words. I didn't know who I really was or what I could really accomplish. Right now I feel more excited, more alive, more *good* about myself than I have in years.''

Suddenly Rafe burst into her thoughts. If she felt excited and alive it was at least in part because of him, she knew. Because the moment they'd kissed she had felt like a new woman. And even when he'd abruptly walked out on her, that feeling hadn't changed. Prince Charming kissing Sleeping Beauty hadn't done a more effective job of awakening a woman.

Ironically, just as Caroline was thinking about Rafe, Marcia mentioned him.

"You know, I was worried about how you'd do after seeing Rafe again. But you seem to have recovered completely."

Looking at her friend guiltily, Caroline admitted, "I went out with him."

"What! And you didn't tell me? When? What happened?"

Caroline smiled wryly. "I take it you want to hear all the sordid details?"

"Of course."

Caroline tried to make her voice matter-of-fact, as if her date really wasn't as important as Marcia seemed to assume it was. "Well, he called one evening and we went out to dinner."

"Where?"

"The Pheasant Run Restaurant up in Oakhurst."

Marcia grinned impishly. "Nothing but the best. I like that. Shows a little class. So what happened?"

"Marcia, you understand that the only reason I went out with him was because I couldn't think of a polite excuse to get out of it."

"Sure." Her tone indicated that she didn't believe that for one minute.

"All I'm interested in is having a civil relationship with the man, so that when we run into each other, as we're bound to, it won't be a big deal emotionally."

"Right. So what happened?" Marcia repeated.

"We had dinner."

Marcia's voice was sarcastic. "No kidding? What a surprising thing to do at a restaurant. Seriously, Carrie, what happened?"

"We seemed to get along okay at first. Then he became rather cool and the evening ended quite abruptly."

"Did you say or do something that bothered him?"

"Not that I'm aware of. It was strange."

Then, skipping over the kiss that she couldn't bring herself to discuss, she finished, "Anyway, I don't expect to see him again. And I certainly don't want to."

Marcia shot her a curious look. "Are you sure about that?"

"Positive."

They were at Marcia's house by then, in the old, tree-shaded neighborhood called Fig Garden. Marcia's home was a gracious two story red brick house on a large lot overflowing with trees, shrubs and flowers. It was very pleasant and homey, exactly the sort of place Caroline wanted to have some day.

As they got out of the car, Marcia said, "Come on in for a cup of coffee. I may even have some oatmeal cookies, if the kids haven't finished them off."

"Now that's an invitation I can't refuse."

In the sunny breakfast nook with huge windows overlooking the sparkling pool in the backyard, Caroline sat down while Marcia made the coffee. While it was perking, she checked the cookie jar and came up with two cookies.

"Well, they left something at any rate," she said with a grin.

She put the cookies on a small plate, and when the coffee was ready, she poured two cups, adding sugar for herself and cream for Caroline.

Watching her oldest and dearest friend, Caroline finally decided to ask a question that had concerned her for some time.

"Why haven't you started dating?"

Marcia's deep-blue eyes were startled. Clearly, she hadn't expected the question and wasn't sure how to answer it. Finally, she said slowly, "Maybe no one has asked me."

Caroline's voice was warm with caring and concern. "Maybe you haven't encouraged anyone to ask you."

Marcia sighed heavily and cupped her hands around the warm white porcelain cup that held her coffee. "You're right. I haven't. You see, Carl and I were very happy together. After twenty years it was better than ever. Do you understand?"

"Of course, I do. He was a wonderful man." Caroline's voice softened with tenderness, "But, Marcia, he's gone. It's been four years. You've mourned long enough."

"It isn't that, honestly. I'm not in mourning any longer. I can look at our photo albums and go through his things and feel happy remembering our time together. All the fun we had...the love. It makes me feel good now, not sad. But..."

"But what?"

"I was only eighteen when I married him. He was my high-school sweetheart. I spent my entire adult life with him. I don't know what other men are like. I wouldn't know how to behave with another man."

"Marcia, I understand your nervousness. Boy, do I. When I went out with Rafe I felt awkward and gauche, just like I did on my very first date at fifteen. You'd think we'd get over worrying about our makeup being perfect and not saying dumb things, but we don't. No matter who I go out with next time, I'll feel just as nervous. But you know, you've gotta test the water sometime.''

"I know. And I will—eventually.''

Caroline didn't press the issue. She didn't believe in telling other people how to run their lives, especially when she couldn't seem to do as good a job with her own as she would like.

For a moment she and Marcia sat there quietly, nibbling on their cookies and slowly sipping their coffee.

Then Marcia said tentatively, "Carrie, about Rafe…''

At Caroline's wary look, she hurried on, "Now don't go all stubborn on me. I just wanted to say that I've run into him quite a lot over the years, and frankly I kind of like him.''

Caroline couldn't contain a dry smile. "The man's attractive. I never said otherwise.''

"I'm not referring to the fact that on a scale of one to ten, he's an eleven. I mean he's not a jerk. I've never known him to make a pass at a married woman. He has his standards, even if he is a bit of a philanderer. And he single-handedly started a halfway house for delinquent boys. Plus he's really respected in the business community.''

"I'm sure he is. Success is always respected.''

"Yes, he's a success, and he's certainly no pushover, from what Carl used to tell me. They had some business dealings, you know. Carl said he was absolutely straight, there was nothing shady about anything he did. His word could be depended on.''

"Marcia, what are you getting at?''

"Maybe there's an explanation for his behavior when you got pregnant.''

Caroline's expression was tight and angry. This was a subject she didn't like to discuss and Marcia knew it. If

Marcia wasn't such an old friend, Caroline would have simply told her to mind her own business and left in a huff. As it was, it was all she could do to contain her anger.

"You know what happened that summer. When I told Rafe I was pregnant, he was less than thrilled. He never tried to get in touch with me after that, and he didn't respond to the note I wrote him. And during all these years that he's been such an upstanding citizen, he's never tried to find out about his daughter."

Marcia said quickly, "Okay, I'm sorry. I wouldn't have brought it up, but if there's a chance you two might get involved again....

"There's no chance of that. I was just trying to be civil to him, and considering the way the evening ended, even that isn't going to be possible. So let's just drop it."

Marcia didn't say a word for one long, tense moment. Then she gave Caroline a shy smile. "I don't have another cookie to offer, thanks to my kids' bottomless stomachs. But I can get you another cup of coffee, if you'd like."

Caroline's angry expression slowly softened. Finally she met Marcia's tentative smile. "Thanks. I'd like another cup of coffee. Now, about tomorrow morning..."

They talked for a while about their plans, and by the time Caroline left, she and Marcia were comfortable with each other again. But as Caroline drove home, she was extremely irritated. Rafael Marin always seemed to cause trouble for her. He was even causing arguments between her and Marcia now. She hoped he would never show up again. But if he did she would have to make it absolutely clear to him that she wanted nothing to do with him.

Nothing.

The next day was Saturday. Marcia's son and daughter, Jason and Jill, twins who shared her dark hair and bright-blue eyes, helped unload the trailer. Then they returned it while Marcia and Caroline started wallpapering. The shop was small and almost a perfect square, with only one door in the front and another in the back leading to a small workroom and bathroom. The front of the store was almost all windows. There were no awkward angles or fixtures to work around, so, as Caroline had promised, it wasn't difficult hanging the wallpaper.

Marcia and Caroline had picked out a gray-and-mauve flowered print that would provide just the right old-fashioned background for the dolls. While they hung the wallpaper, Jason and Jill painted the window and door frames a soft gray.

It was a happy way to work, with lots of joking and teasing. Jason and Jill, who were both going off to college in the fall, were clearly relieved to see that their mother would have something to fill her time now that her nest was going to be empty.

By the end of the afternoon, everything was ready for the shelves to be hung. Jason and Jill returned home to get ready for their respective dates, and Marcia left to talk to the man who was making the sign for the shop. Caroline was alone, contemplating the shelves.

While she had done a lot of painting and wallpapering in her time, she'd done almost no carpentry work. Looking at the shelves, she felt rather overwhelmed. They had agreed they would try to do most of the work themselves to save money, but she was beginning to think they might have to hire a carpenter after all.

Still, she decided with a sigh, she might as well at least try it herself first. Maybe hammers, nails and brackets would turn out to be less daunting than they looked.

Picking up a hammer and nail, she started to work.

"You really should have a plan first."

The voice from the doorway behind her was light and casual. But the timbre was characteristic and unforgettable.

Caroline swung around, as the atmosphere of the room changed with a new force flowing into it.

Chapter Five

Even before she turned around to face the man standing in the open doorway, she knew who it was. He seemed to always catch her in jeans and a T-shirt, she thought irritably. At least this time he was dressed similarly, though his jeans weren't as old and faded as hers, and the blue work shirt rolled up to his elbows was crisp and clean.

She said the first thing that came into her mind. "How did you know where I was?"

"I've been calling all day. Finally, I tried Marcia's house, thinking she might know where you were. Jill told me about the shop."

He glanced around. "Did you do all this yourselves?"

She nodded.

"I'm impressed. But you know you're about to ruin it by putting up the shelves wrong."

Caroline felt anger welling up within her. She knew deep inside that it had to do with what had happened on their date, but she preferred to focus on what was happening between them now. Who the hell was he, anyway, to come waltzing in, smugly telling her what to do?

"I've managed to get this far without your advice. I think I can manage quite all right."

He leaned against the door frame and crossed his arms. The expression on his dark, compelling face was perfectly innocent.

"Okay. Go right ahead. I'll just watch."

He had succeeded in rattling her composure in more ways than one. As she turned back to the wall, she felt totally confused. What if he was right, that she should have some sort of plan worked out in advance before putting up the shelves? And how did one go about making sure the shelves were perfectly even, anyway?

Turning back to him, she asked in a tone that was barely polite, "I suppose you're an expert carpenter?"

"No. But I started out in real estate in the construction end. I can frame a house. And I can sure as hell hang a shelf."

The mental image of Rafe doing construction work, stripped to the waist as construction workers often were in the summer, his dark skin made even more bronze by the unrelenting sun, was erotic in the extreme. It jolted Caroline, and wreaked havoc with her determination to resist him.

She gave up.

Holding out the hammer toward him, almost as a peace offering, she said, "Okay. It's all yours."

He grinned, and this time his eyes were warm with genuine humor. For one brief, fleeting moment he looked startlingly like the seventeen-year-old boy whom she'd loved so desperately. The boy who had been so vulnerable beneath his brashness, so incredibly tender in spite of his physical strength.

Caroline felt her heart turn over with a soft thud, and her breath caught in her throat. At that moment she was more vividly aware of him physically than ever before. His quicksilver-gray eyes, his husky voice, his lean, strong body seemed to hold a promise... a promise of ecstasy...

She took a vigorous hold of herself and tried to smile casually.

"So how do we go about this?"

He took the hammer from her hand and set it down.

"Before we pound in so much as a single nail, we decide how you want the shelves to be arranged. Dolls are the only things going on them, I take it?"

She nodded. "Most of them are going in glassed-in cases, actually. I just thought it would look nice to have a few shelves, especially these clear, acrylic ones, with some dolls arranged casually to catch the eye of people looking in from outside."

"Good idea. From outside, people won't be able to see them too clearly in those cases. You've got to entice people into the shop before you can sell them anything, you see."

"You don't say." Her tone held wry amusement.

"All right, I'll stop trying to tell you your business. I'll settle for showing you how to put up shelves."

Holding up the longest shelf, he continued, "I think this one should go on this wall, and the two shorter shelves should be arranged on slightly different levels on the opposite wall. Okay?"

"Okay."

He pulled a small tape measure out of his back pocket.

"Do you always carry that with you?" Caroline asked curiously.

"Not always. I've been known to attend a concert without it. But in my business I never know when I'm going to need to do a quick measuring job."

He quickly measured the height for the shelves and marked the correct places lightly with a pencil.

"Now we put in the brackets first, making sure they're very secure so the whole thing doesn't come tumbling down while you're in the midst of making a big sale."

Caroline smiled in spite of herself. "I wouldn't want that to happen."

Her face was raised to Rafe's as he stood only a few feet from her. Through the big front windows of the shop, the light from the setting sun fell on her pale skin and her full, soft mouth and made her brown eyes glint as if they were made of molten gold.

She wasn't aware of the effect, or of the blush that suffused her cheeks when his light, amused expression slowly changed to one of highly charged sensuality.

"No," he said slowly, carefully, as if barely trusting himself to speak. "No, you wouldn't want that to happen."

Suddenly Caroline felt she had to say something, anything to break the pregnant silence that fell between them.

"Why . . . why did you leave the door open?"

"Because for some reason I couldn't breathe."

He nearly choked on the last word.

Then he dropped the brackets that he'd been holding and reaching out, pulled Caroline toward him. His arms enfolded her as she stepped into them and wrapped her own arms around his neck. The first startled flicker of surprise in her look gave way to pleasure as their lips met.

The kiss was unexpectedly gentle. His lips brushed hers lightly, teasingly, tantalizing her with their taste and feel. It was as if he knew that she was his for the taking, and he could afford to take his time with her. He was playing with her, as a cat plays with a mouse, only she was enjoying the game every bit as much as he was.

When her mouth parted slightly, his tongue slid in, seeking her moist warmth. Inside her, a thousand butterflies took flight, and she was suffused with a lilting happiness.

Even when the kiss ended, he continued to hold her, hugging her against him as if he was afraid to let her go.

She rested her cheek against his chest and murmured softly, "Why did you walk away that night?"

His own voice was nearly as soft as hers, his expression transfixed with tenderness. "Because I wanted you too much." He brushed her forehead with his lips. "Why did you let me go?"

. "For the same reason."

She wasn't angry now, or defensive. She looked up at him utterly happy, her lips parted with wonderment and her eyes shining with laughter.

She went on, "I told myself I would have nothing to do with you."

He looked down at her covetously, smiling a little, his firm chin drawn down. "I wouldn't call this nothing." He bent to kiss her again, and this time it wasn't nearly so gentle.

He was shaking slightly, as was she, and it almost seemed that she could feel their hearts beating together.

When they finally pulled apart again, he said, "I'll take you on a picnic tomorrow."

It wasn't an invitation, but a fait accompli. Yet she couldn't find it in her to resent the presumption that she would go.

Releasing her, he said in a voice that wasn't entirely under control, "Now, about those shelves . . ."

When Marcia walked in a few minutes later, she was startled to find Rafe putting up the last shelf, and Caroline watching quietly.

"Rafe! What a nice surprise. Has Caroline put you to work?"

"Yup. And I'm just about finished. There." He put the last shelf in place. Then, glancing around, he added, "It's really looking nice. I wish both of you the best of luck."

Marcia grinned happily. "Thanks. We'll need it. The guy who's making our sign went on at great length about all the small businesses he knows of that have gone under lately."

"Don't listen to pessimists. Well, I'd better be going. Nice seeing you again, Marcia."

"You too, Rafe."

To Caroline he said simply, "Twelve o'clock?"

She nodded and he left.

The moment he closed the door behind him, Marcia whirled around to face Caroline. It was all she could do to contain herself until she was sure Rafe was well out of hearing.

"All right. What's up?"

Caroline sighed. "Forget everything I told you. I'm a liar. And what's worse, I'm a fool."

"I knew it! You two can't stay away from each other."

"That's a fairly accurate way of putting it. When I'm away from him, I'm full of firm resolve. But the minute I look at him, that resolve goes right out the window."

"Well, judging from the way he was looking at you, the feeling's mutual."

"Marcia, don't try to turn this into true romance. I admit there's a strong physical attraction between us. There always has been. But that's all it is."

"Whatever you say."

"Marcia."

"I'm just agreeing with you. Why are you upset?"

"I'm not upset," Caroline snapped. Then, realizing that she was being ridiculous, she laughed at herself and shook her head in exasperation. "I must be crazy."

"You are. You're crazy about Rafe. Always have been, always will be. I take it you're seeing him tomorrow."

Caroline nodded. "We're going on a picnic. That sounds innocent enough, doesn't it?"

Marcia laughed. "Sure. To tell you the truth, the way the sparks were flying between you two, I don't think a date in the middle of Times Square on New Year's Eve could be entirely innocent."

Caroline's expression grew concerned. She knew that Marcia was right. Now that Rafe was gone and she was coming to her senses again, she began to wish she hadn't agreed to go on that picnic. Till now they had been together only in public places, which provided a certain degree of safety. But a picnic out in the country somewhere, just the two of them, alone...

Rafe may have talked about containing his emotions, but the fierce passion that had once leveled her resistance was still there, barely held in check. Rafael Marin wasn't the kind of man to stop at tantalizing kisses.

And the way her body responded to him, she wasn't at all sure she would want him to stop.

Heat shimmered on the dark asphalt of Highway 41. It was another hot day, nearly 100 degrees by noon and bound to get hotter. But in the quietly powerful Jaguar, it was cool and pleasant. A wicker picnic basket and red and black plaid blanket sat on the back seat.

In the front, Rafe concentrated on driving. He enjoyed driving and did it well. It was a form of total relaxation, the only one he knew. Everything else he did, whether it was work or play, had an element of competition in it. And when he competed, he meant to win.

It had been that way with sports in high school. That was the only arena where he had to be accepted as the equal, and sometimes the superior, of the people he envied. People like Caroline.

He glanced at her now, sitting next to him, looking out the window at the gently rolling countryside they were passing through on the way up to the mountains. She looked incredibly lovely in an aquamarine T-shirt and white cotton slacks that emphasized her long legs.

Tiny gold hoops in her ears were her only jewelry. He wondered why she wore so little jewelry and finally decided that she probably simply couldn't afford it. But she was the type of woman who should wear stunning jewelry, he thought. Eighteen carat gold to match the golden pinpoints of light in her eyes. Real stones like diamonds and emeralds, because nothing cheap should ever touch her exquisite porcelain skin.

Caroline looked at him and for an instant their eyes locked. What he saw in her eyes sent his pulse racing and started a slow burning fire deep inside him, a fire that he needed to let rage out of control.

Today, he thought. It had to be today, because he couldn't wait any longer. And neither could she.

Just past Shaver Lake, Rafe turned off the main highway onto a smaller road. After driving for a few miles, he turned off again, this time onto a graveled lane marked Private, No Trespassing.

When Caroline shot him a questioning look, he said easily, "I own this property. I always meant to build a vacation home on it someday, but I never seem to get around to it."

They drove for a mile, deep into the forest, finally coming out into a small meadow stretching to a cliff. Wildflowers dotted the meadow with pinpoints of blue, lavender, yellow and orange in the pale-green grass of the meadow. At one end of it a tiny brook, only a few feet across and a few inches deep, meandered in and out of the trees that circled the meadow.

They got out of the car, and while Rafe saw to the picnic things, Caroline walked to the edge of the cliff. Below, and in the distance, she saw Shaver Lake shimmering a deep blue on this warm, crystal clear midsummer day. Behind the meadow were the towering peaks of the magnificent Sierra Nevadas, breathtaking in their jagged majesty.

"What a fabulous view!"

Rafe smiled at her as he set down the picnic basket and blanket nearby. "That's why I bought it. And it's absolutely private. No one else for miles around."

Caroline looked startled, her composure shaken.

He knew what she was thinking. That the first place they had made love was a mountain meadow. He had been determined not to take her in the back seat of a car or a cheap motel room, their only alternatives. She wasn't just another conquest. And even more importantly, she was totally innocent. He wanted her first experience with making love to be wonderful, a memory she could treasure with happiness instead of a sense of shame.

And so he'd brought her to a meadow not unlike this one that summer they were seventeen. What happened had altered both their lives forever.

Now he looked at her, standing before him with a touching combination of hesitation and openness. And for the first time since he had decided that he was going to break her heart, he wondered if he could go through with it.

"I'll... I'll spread out the blanket over there in the shade," he finally said.

"Okay." Her voice was just slightly tremulous. "I'll unpack the basket."

When the blanket was spread out in the cool shade of a leafy oak tree, Rafe sat down on it. Caroline knelt down on the edge of it and began unpacking the picnic basket.

"You've brought a feast." As she named the contents, she set them out on the blanket. "Cheese...mmm, Brie, my favorite... grapes... French bread... chicken, of course, what would a picnic be without chicken? And strawberries."

"And wine," Rafe finished, taking a bottle of Chardonnay out of a tall, round side compartment on the basket. He uncorked it to let it breathe, then set it back in the compartment.

Caroline set out white china plates rimmed with silver, heavy silverware and two tall, elegant glasses of fine crystal. "This is a formal picnic, I see," she teased.

"Of course."

He laid back on the blanket, propping up his head on his hand.

"Shall I serve?" Caroline asked with mock subservience.

"Please do."

She put a little of everything on both plates, then handed one to Rafe. Then she poured wine for both of them. As she handed Rafe his glass, he raised it to hers. "A toast."

She held her glass toward his and waited, clearly curious what the toast would be.

"To the simple things in life," he said with a wry grin.

She laughed appreciatively, then touched her glass to his. A ringing sound, as clear and high as only the finest crystal can make, sang out in the quiet of the meadow. The wine, with its hint of sweetness, was delicious.

They ate in companionable silence for a while. The Brie was smooth and creamy, the chicken crisp, the strawberries sweet and juicy. Yet neither Rafe nor Caroline's attention was entirely on the food. They kept glancing at each other, then looking away, ostensibly concentrating on the food.

When she had finished, Caroline leaned back on one elbow and took a final sip of wine.

"Full?" Rafe asked.

She nodded. "It's so warm today, even up at this altitude. I can imagine what it's like down in the valley."

"It's a typical valley day in early August. Hotter than hell and just enough smog to make everyone stop taking potshots at L.A." He yawned suddenly, then smiled in embarrassment. "Between the heat and the food, not to mention the wine, I'm feeling rather drowsy."

"I thought you seemed tired."

He didn't tell her that he was tired because he'd hardly slept the night before. An uncomfortable combination of conscience and desire had kept him tossing and turning.

"Why don't you take a nap? I won't mind."

He smiled tiredly. "It would be rather rude to fall asleep in front of you."

"Don't be ridiculous." She rose and added, "I'm going exploring. If you're asleep when I get back, I promise not to wake you."

He lay back on the blanket and watched through heavy lidded eyes as she walked over to the brook. Taking off her sandals, she rolled up her pant legs to the knee, then waded in the cold mountain water. Occasionally she bent over to pick up an interesting looking stone from the bottom of the brook.

As his eyes slowly closed, he thought how incredibly lovely she looked. . . .

Caroline looked back over her shoulder at Rafe's sleeping form. Wearing a short sleeved gray shirt and matching slacks, he lay stretched out on the blanket, his head resting on one arm. Seeing him lying there so peacefully, looking unexpectedly vulnerable, made her smile tenderly to herself.

Then, turning back to the stream, she continued looking for small rocks that had been polished to a glossy sheen. The water swirled around her ankles, ice-cold and refreshing in the heat.

When she found a particularly lovely piece of rose quartz, she felt as delighted as a kid and happily dropped it into her pocket.

After a few minutes she left the stream, put her sandals back on and walked into the forest. For a half hour or so she wandered in the shady depths, occasionally picking flowers. By the time she returned to the meadow, she had an impressive bouquet of wildflowers clutched in her hands.

Quietly, trying not to make a sound, she went to the blanket where Rafe still lay asleep. Taking the empty wine bottle she went to the stream, rinsed it out, then filled it and stuck the flowers in it. She returned to the blanket, put the makeshift vase back into the wine bottle compartment of the picnic basket and sat down without making a sound.

She had never seen Rafe asleep before. Feeling slightly guilty, yet too curious to resist, she watched him. Asleep, his expression was soft and appealing. The wariness and the defensiveness were gone. Caroline was surprised to find herself feeling protective toward him, nearly holding her breath so that she wouldn't wake him from a sleep he clearly needed. But his was the deep sleep of physical fatigue, and even when a bluejay squawked overhead, Rafe didn't wake.

The sun moved across the sky and the shadows from the trees lengthened on the meadow. Finally, growing tired herself, Caroline lay down beside Rafe. Just as she did so, he woke up.

They lay only a foot apart, their eyes locked. In an instant, Rafe was wide awake, all tiredness gone from his expression. His eyes glinted as they bored into hers. And though he didn't say a word, or make the slightest move toward her, she *knew*.

This was the time. This meadow, the place. There would be no more waiting.

Reaching out, he pulled her into his arms. She felt his strong arms encircle her and she didn't resist. When she had agreed to come today, she'd known what might happen. From their kiss of the day before, it had been inevitable.

But this time with Rafe she wasn't a naive girl. She was an experienced woman. She was too honest to pretend reluctance, too filled with desire for him to be coy. And so she pressed her body against his and felt the soft, curling hair on his chest where his gray shirt was unbuttoned.

As her hips lightly brushed against his, she felt the hard, throbbing pressure between his legs. At the same moment, her mouth reached up to his and they kissed long and deeply.

He slipped one leg between hers, pulling her even more tightly against him, and she relaxed completely in his embrace, the last vestige of resistance melting away. He groaned deep in his throat, a low, animal sound, and Caroline felt her body stir in response.

She wanted him. God, how she wanted him. She had wanted him all this time and had been foolish enough to try to deny it. Now, she couldn't deny any of her feelings for him... the tenderness, the hunger, the need.

When his lips finally left hers, she whispered his name, *"Rafael,"* loving the sound of it.

"My lady," he answered in a deep, dusky voice. "My heart's delight... Caroline..."

It was almost magic the way their clothes were removed so quickly and effortlessly. She lay beneath him, her pale skin contrasting sensuously with his bronze coloring. His body was as hard and muscled as she remembered, his hands at once strong and gentle.

Cupping her oval face in his hands, he whispered, "You're more beautiful than ever."

She smiled shyly, more touched than she could possibly express by the obvious sincerity of the compliment. She wanted him to find her as desirable as she found him.

Slowly, with almost excruciating deliberation, his hands began to explore her body, pausing to pay special attention to the secret places he'd once known intimately. Her back arched at his touch, her breathing grew quicker.

At the same time, his lips brushed her cheek, her throat, the hollow between her breasts.

She twined her fingers in his hair as his head dipped beneath her breasts. A tiny moan of pleasure escaped her lips.

"I want you," she whispered. "I want you so...."

He moved to hover over her, one arm on either side of her. "I want you sweetheart. I want you here, now."

She smiled up at him as her arms encircled his back. Implicit in her smile was an invitation that didn't need to be spoken.

Slowly, with infinite gentleness, they were joined. Then came a rocking motion as her body began to move with his, at first awkwardly, then in perfect unison. As the movement grew faster, more urgent, her nails dug into his back. She wanted to draw him even closer to her, to become part of him.

His lips were on hers again while his hands pulled up her hips to meet his.

And then came the fire, a tiny spark at first, quickly growing, igniting both together, making their bodies as taut as bowstrings stretched to the limit. Somehow the tautness didn't break, but held, their bodies growing rigid against each other, as Caroline was filled with wave after wave of hot fire....

Afterward, they lay in each other's arms, part of the blanket pulled over their naked bodies.

Even after coming back down to earth, Caroline still couldn't believe how good it had been. It was even more exciting, more fulfilling than it had been when they were young. But was it the same for Rafe? she wondered, as a sudden doubt assailed her. For her, the experience was almost shattering. But was it so for him? Or was it just a physical release with no accompanying emotion?

She turned to face him, seeking in his eyes the answer to those devastating questions.

A slow smile spread across his rugged face and his silver eyes held all the tenderness in the world. "You've made my heart your own," he whispered.

She sighed softly. It was all right.

Then he noticed the flowers in the wine bottle. Reaching over, he took one and gently laid it across her breasts.

She smiled. "What on earth are you doing?"

He took another and laid it across her stomach. "Making you a wood nymph." His tone was teasing and there was an amused glint in his eyes.

"Are you, now?"

"Yup."

One by one he took the flowers until almost every one was strewn across her naked body.

"You're being very silly, Rafael Marin," she said with a grin.

"You make me feel silly. Among other things."

Taking the last flower from the bottle, he brushed it lightly across Caroline's cheek. The petals felt silky smooth and sensuous.

"At this moment I am absolutely happy," she said softly, her voice tinged with a sense of wonder.

His eyes met and held hers. "At this moment, so am I."

Her arms went around his neck. "You should build that house here. This is a very special place."

"It is now. Every time I come back here I'll remember this."

Caroline knew that whether or not she ever came back to this place, she, too, would remember this day.

Forever.

Chapter Six

"All right, what happened?"

Marcia stood on the threshold of the shop, waiting impatiently, as Caroline walked up the next morning, holding a box filled with dolls.

Caroline walked past her, looking half embarrassed and half pleased. "I don't suppose it would do any good to pretend I have no idea what you're referring to?"

Marcia shook her head. "None at all."

Taking the box from Caroline, she sat it down, then led Caroline to a pair of folding chairs. They sat down facing each other, and Marcia ordered, "Okay, shoot."

"Well, we went on a picnic."

"Where?"

"Up past Shaver, at some property Rafe owns. He's going to build a vacation home on it eventually. It was really beautiful, a lovely meadow overlooking the lake below. A little stream meandering through the trees..."

"Carrie, I couldn't care less about the property. I want to know what happened with you two?"

Caroline's breezy smile softened with remembrance. Finally, she said slowly, "What happened is that I put the past behind me. I've lived with anger and bitterness too long. I'm ready to move on now."

Marcia reached out to hug her friend affectionately. "Oh, I'm so glad to hear you say that. It would be wonderful if things could finally work out for you and Rafe."

Caroline's expression sobered and the glow in her golden eyes dimmed almost imperceptibly. "Marcia, don't start assuming we're going to live happily ever after. This is real life, not a fairy tale. Rafe may look like Prince Charming, but he's actually a very complicated man with more than his fair share of faults. And I'm certainly not playing at being Cinderella any longer. I've learned my lessons too well."

The expression in Marcia's blue eyes was tinged with sadness. "I know what you're saying, Carrie. When Carl died I thought life was a cruel joke. There are still times when I think so—when there's a serious problem with the kids and I have to handle it alone. Or when I'm home alone on Saturday night and I wish I had someone to go out and have a good time with."

She was no longer smiling now, and there was a grimness in her expression that fell just short of desperation. Caroline recognized it all too well, because she had felt that way many times herself in the months since Edward had left her. At first it had been panic, then it had slowly given way to intense disillusionment. Finally it had settled into a realistic acceptance of life as it was instead of as she wished it would be.

And then Rafe had come along. And suddenly there was real excitement in her life. And real joy.

Marcia was silent for a long moment, then went on, "Whatever happens between you and Rafe, enjoy the present. It's so rare in life to be given a second chance. You and Rafe have been given one at a time when you both need it."

Caroline smiled dryly. "I admit my ego needed a boost. And my poor, battered heart needed some T.L.C. But from what I hear, Rafe was doing quite well."

"He made a lot of money and went through one gorgeous girl after another, if that's what you mean. But he wasn't doing all that well."

"Why do you say that?"

Marcia leaned back in her chair and was quiet for a moment as she gave careful consideration to the question. Finally, she said, "I've always sensed he was deeply unhappy. And one night something happened that really made me think so."

"What?" Caroline leaned forward, intensely curious about this unexpected view of Rafe.

"Well, Carl and I were at a big social affair. All the movers and shakers in Clovis were there. And Rafe was in the thick of things. He had just started to be a big contributor to local politics, so, of course, he was in a position of power. People were kissing up to him outrageously."

"He must have enjoyed that, considering where he came from," Caroline couldn't resist interjecting.

"Oh, I'm sure he did enjoy it on one level. But I could tell that the fawning and insincerity really bothered him. His date was absolutely stunning. And she was the daughter of some bigwig, to boot."

"So he had it all that night."

"Yes. But at one point I was talking to him and he said, 'If I lost everything tomorrow, you and Carl are the only people in this room who would give me the time of day.' I made some polite remark about his date obviously being crazy about him, and he replied, 'If I was still pounding nails, she'd look at me like I was dirt.' His voice was more hurt than angry. That was the only time he ever talked to me so openly, without being very guarded. But I've never forgotten it.''

He hadn't talked that openly to her, Caroline realized. Except for one or two rare moments, when she'd sensed pain and vulnerability in him, he had been completely guarded. In all their conversations, they'd almost never touched on really personal matters. She had no idea how he felt about anything except money. And considering what Marcia had told her about his financial contribution to a boys' shelter, he was clearly more complicated in that regard as well.

They had shared the most erotic experience of her life the day before when they'd made love with abandon and highly charged passion in a mountain meadow. She knew his body intimately, as he knew hers. But she didn't know his mind. Or his heart.

It was a sobering realization.

How could she have behaved as wantonly as she'd done with him, as she'd never done with any other man, when he was really a stranger in so many ways?

But she knew the answer all too well. He fired her blood and ravaged her senses. He made her feel gloriously alive.

A small sigh escaped her. Enough of this, she decided abruptly. She was entirely too caught up with Rafe. She had a business to attend to. Forcing a smile that was more lighthearted than she felt, she said to Marcia, "Let's get to work. We've got a small fortune to make, remember?''

Marcia grinned. "I remember. By the way, have you told Marina what we're doing?"

"Yes. I talked to her over the phone recently and told her that I was going Looney Tunes in my old age and having delusions of being a tycoon. Actually, she was very excited about it."

"So were Jason and Jill. They think it'll keep me from bugging them about writing home often when they leave for college. And if I'm successful, they can hit me up for new cars."

Caroline grinned. "I know what you mean. I think Marina sees it the same way. A nice little hobby for Mom to keep me from bugging her. I can't talk to her without asking why she's working as a waitress and living in a house without plumbing, after we spent a fortune putting her through college."

"So she's still living in Big Sur?"

"Yeah. And writing. I asked her to move back here with me, but she politely declined. Said she's going to rough it out there on her own until she can make it as a novelist."

"Good for her. I admire her determination. Oh, I forgot to tell you, our business license will be ready by the fifteenth. We can open then."

"Good. Let's take out an ad in the paper—'Grand Opening,' etc. Maybe even offer a doll as a door prize."

"Good idea."

"And I thought we should take out a small ad in the mail order section at the back of *Dolls* Magazine."

"What's that?"

Caroline took a copy of the magazine out of the box she'd brought in and handed it to Marcia. "It's for doll collectors," she explained.

As Marcia thumbed through it, she said excitedly, "If we could get a mail-order business going on the side, that could be very lucrative."

"Yes, but how will we fill all the orders? I can only make so many dolls."

"I've been giving that some thought."

Caroline grinned. "I suppose you intend to lock me in that tiny back room with a year's worth of doll supplies and never let me see the light of day."

"Not a bad idea. Except I doubt that Rafe would go along with it. It looks like you'll be needing at least some time for a personal life."

"True. There's more to life than porcelain and lace."

"Well, I remembered what you said about that Hmong family—the boy who helped you paint, and his mother who's sewing your drapes. I read an article recently about the Hmongs, and apparently some of them are terrific at sewing and a variety of arts and crafts. Once we start doing well, we could hire some of those women to help make the dolls."

"Marcia, that's a fantastic idea!"

"Well, don't look so surprised. I can do more than bake a mean lasagna, you know."

Caroline laughed. "I know. What's especially nice about this idea is that it would really help the Hmongs. That boy, Tran, was telling me that many of them are still having a hard time finding work."

"That's something you and I can relate to."

"Oh, yes. Well, that takes one worry off my mind. I laid awake half the night worrying about what we would do if we weren't successful. And I laid awake the other half worrying about what we would do if we were."

Marcia was exuberant with confidence. "Well, stop worrying. Our only problem is going to be deciding how to spend all the money we'll make."

"Before we can spend it, we have to make it. Let's unpack these dolls and put them in the cases."

As Marcia started to take the carefully wrapped dolls out of their tissue paper, she went on with growing excitement, "And eventually maybe we could expand to include other things, like really special stuffed animals, music boxes, maybe imported dolls. . . ."

"Marcia!" Caroline interrupted with a laugh.

"Hey, I'm only thinking big."

"Well as Robert Redford said to Paul Newman in *Butch Cassidy and the Sundance Kid*, 'you just keep right on thinking. That's what you do best!' "

By the end of the day, they'd arranged all the dolls in the glass-fronted cases and on the shelves, and organized the store room and tiny bathroom. After deciding to spend the next day shopping for decorations for the shop, they locked up and went home.

Caroline drove her small red Honda Civic down Bullard Avenue through some of the most expensive residential areas in Fresno. They were definitely in the right area, she realized. If only these well-to-do people would be interested enough to come into the shop, she was sure they'd like what they found.

But if they stayed away in droves, as she secretly feared, well, when the three-month lease was up, The Dollhouse would be out of business. Marcia could always go back to the dress shop where she'd worked. Or simply stay home if she chose. She didn't have to earn a living.

But Caroline did. If their risky venture failed, she'd be completely broke and desperately in need of a job, fast. Though she downplayed the importance of the success of the shop when she was with Marcia, the truth was that it was absolutely crucial to her.

After twenty minutes, she turned right onto Clovis Avenue. This was the main street of Clovis, a busy four-lane thoroughfare that passed low buildings and small shopping centers. Clovis was no longer the small town it had once been; it actually merged with Fresno, a medium sized city to the west. But it retained a western flavor that reflected the rural, agriculture-oriented ambience of the valley. Pickups were seen here more often than Mercedes. And cowboy boots weren't an affectation but a practical choice.

Many of the storefronts were done western style, and the word "rodeo" was used often in the names of stores and shopping centers. This was a frank acknowledgement of the popularity and importance of the annual Clovis Rodeo held each spring.

It was a far cry from the cosmopolitan ambience of San Francisco, with its towering downtown skyline, and heavy emphasis on Culture with a capital *C*. The San Joaquin Valley was the richest agricultural area in the world. And while everyone in it wasn't necessarily a farmer, in many ways most people's livelihoods depended on how well the crops did.

Yet Caroline didn't miss the city. The valley might not have the gourmet restaurants, haute couture shops and myriad cultural offerings San Francisco did, but what it did have were warm, down-to-earth people, orchards that bloomed in the spring, fields and vineyards and livestock. And traditional values that reflected the people's closeness to the land.

And Rafe. Most of all, Rafe.

As Caroline walked into her house she felt strangely nervous. She'd been too busy all day to give much thought to Rafe. But as she tossed her purse on a table, then went into her bedroom to change into shorts, he was all she could think of.

Going into the kitchen, she poured a glass of iced tea, then went out onto the patio where she stretched out on a lounge chair. She closed her eyes tiredly and remembered the previous evening. They had stopped for dinner at a small, unpretentious Mexican restaurant that featured home-made tortillas and the spiciest chili con carne Caroline had tasted in quite a while. Neither had said much, yet it hadn't been an uncomfortable silence.

Then Rafe had dropped her off. He murmured something vague about understanding that she would want to get to bed early since she would be busy at the shop the next day and left.

No good-night kiss.

No, "I'll call you."

Nothing.

At the time Caroline was too caught up in the aftermath of their lovemaking to wonder about his behavior. But now she faced the tiny nagging doubt that had been at the back of her mind all day.

She was sure Rafe had been moved by their lovemaking as she had been. The proof was in his eyes as he looked at her with such wonder, and in his touch, as he explored her body with infinite tenderness. He hadn't just seen to his own pleasure, but to hers as well.

It wasn't just another affair for him. It couldn't be. Even if he was a stranger in so many ways, she couldn't be so far wrong in her judgment about that.

But afterward, she admitted, afterward as they drove down from the mountains, he was quiet. Unusually quiet, even taking into consideration the fact that at the best of times he wasn't overly talkative.

Caroline opened her eyes, took a sip of the cold, lemony tea and glanced at her watch. Eight o'clock. And she hadn't heard from him.

There was a phone at the shop where she'd been all day. He could have reached her there if he'd tried. And even if he was too busy with his own business, surely he should have called her at home by now. She'd been home for half an hour, and the phone hadn't rung once.

She had half expected him to suggest they have dinner together. Clearly, by this late hour, that wasn't going to happen.

Was he going to call, period? she wondered.

And if he didn't? If there was no just-before-bedtime call saying "I'm sorry I couldn't call earlier, I missed you today, when can I see you again?"—what then?

This is ridiculous, Caroline told herself suddenly. She was rapidly sinking into self-doubt and, what was even worse, self-pity. So what if Rafe didn't call today—or tomorrow, for that matter? It didn't mean a thing. Up to now she had only seen him once a week. Obviously, the man was terribly busy.

And besides, there'd been no talk of commitment or even love between them. They were very attracted to each other and they had acted on that attraction. That was all that had happened. It was too early to tell if something more might develop. At this point, fresh from her divorce, with a new business to consider, she wasn't even sure she wanted anything further to develop between them.

And she certainly wasn't going to sit here all night, worrying about what Rafael Marin might or might not do.

Full of high resolve, she went into the kitchen, cooked a big dinner that she didn't particularly want and ate half of it. After taking a long, hot bath that was meant to be relaxing but somehow wasn't, she went to bed with the latest Sidney Sheldon novel.

Rafe sat at the small, elegantly set table, listlessly eyeing his after dinner brandy. He rarely drank anything more than wine with meals, but this night he felt the need for something stimulating. God knows why, he thought dryly. Gayle Gillespie was usually stimulating enough in her own right. She was the most spectacularly beautiful woman in Fresno, with a glossy mane of auburn hair that hung to her waist in sexy disarray, honey-colored skin, and almond-shaped eyes that were so deep-brown they were almost black. Her figure was spectacular, too, as Rafe well knew.

Gayle was the only child of a wealthy real estate developer who had been Rafe's competitor on more than one project, which added to her appeal for him. He suspected that his sometimes bitter rivalry with her father added to his appeal for her, as well.

They were dining on the flagstone patio outside her lavish condominium on the bluffs overlooking the San Joaquin River. The river glistened darkly in the moonlight, and a small breeze wafted in lazily, cooling the warm, early August night.

It should have been a perfect evening. Dinner had been delicious. And Gayle, wearing the filmiest black silk caftan Rafe had ever seen outside a bedroom, was obviously dressed for seduction.

"There's fruit ambrosia for dessert, if you're still hungry," Gayle murmured in the sultry voice that had driven more than one man to distraction.

Rafe shook his head. "No, thanks."

She leaned forward on the table, letting the deep décolletage of the caftan slip even further to reveal a provocative glimpse of full breasts unencumbered by a bra.

"Can I get you anything else, sugar?"

Rafe's mouth curved in the barest hint of a smile. "No, I don't think so."

Gayle cupped her chin in her hands and gave Rafe a long, quizzical stare.

Gently swirling his brandy in the large crystal snifter, Rafe finally took a sip. Then, meeting Gayle's look, he asked with a hint of impatience in his tone, "What are you looking at?"

"I was just trying to decide. It sure isn't the Rafe I know and occasionally love."

"Is that so?"

"That's so."

"What are you getting at, Gayle?"

"You've been somewhere else all evening. Oh, your body's here, all right. Don't get me wrong, normally that would be enough. Ours has never been what you might call an attraction of the intellect."

Rafe laughed shortly. "No, it hasn't."

"But you are *so* out of it tonight, that I don't think you even know I'm here."

"Oh, I know you're here, Gayle. And I know you're wearing absolutely nothing beneath that not very subtle gown."

She grinned wickedly, her eyes flashing. "Now where did subtlety ever get anyone? If you've got it, flaunt it. And Rafe, honey, I've got it."

"Have I ever suggested you didn't?"

"The way you're ignoring me tonight makes me think you've forgotten it. We've had some wild times together, you and I. Let's have some more right now."

As an invitation to sex it had the definite advantage of being completely unambivalent. And it was precisely what Rafe had gone there for. When he had called Gayle the night before and set up the date, he'd assumed they would end up in bed. They always did.

It had seemed like a damned good idea at the time, a way to nullify the unexpectedly profound effect Caroline had on him. Their lovemaking hadn't turned out as he'd planned. She had been as willing, even eager, as he'd expected she would be. What he hadn't expected was how touched emotionally he would be by her.

Instead of the purely physical joining of bodies he'd anticipated, he had been overwhelmed with tenderness for her. When she looked up at him with those golden eyes, he wanted to do more than make love to her. He wanted to love her. And that was a feeling that had to be nipped in the bud.

Even now, with Gayle looking sexy as hell and coming on to him in a manner that would make most men grovel, it was Caroline whom Rafe was thinking of. In his mind's eye he could still see her... wading in the stream, looking like an adorable hoyden... watching him shyly over the rim of her wine glass... rendering passion for passion with a loving generosity of spirit that was immensely touching.

And there was more that he wasn't prepared for. This wasn't the same innocent girl who'd been embarrassed by her own passionate nature.

This was a woman who knew how to love a man thoroughly and well. But, he suspected, a woman who hadn't been loved as thoroughly and well in her marriage. She didn't have to say a word about the inadequacies of her ex-husband. Her startled gratitude at Rafe's sensitivity to her needs was mute testimony to Edward's clumsiness.

The idea that any man wouldn't appreciate and nurture Caroline's immense capacity for passion made Rafe furious. But that anger meant he cared for her. And he couldn't allow that because caring about her wasn't part of the plan. He was supposed to be seducing her, not falling in love with her.

So he'd come to Gayle, hoping that a night of sexual acrobatics with her would wipe away those memories of Caroline. Only it wasn't working.

Because it wasn't Gayle he wanted.

Now, looking at Gayle across the table, he said slowly, "I'm afraid I'm wasting your time tonight."

Gayle's dark eyes narrowed in frustration and disappointment, "What do you mean?"

"I mean I'm going home. I'm sorry, but . . . well, I'm sorry."

As he rose from the table, Gayle stood up and said icily, "Are you trying to make a fool of me?"

Rafe's voice was infinitely patient and kind. "No. You've got it backward. I'm the one being a fool. Don't bother showing me out. I know the way."

A moment later he was out of the house. Behind him, he could still hear the muffled sound of Gayle hurling abuse at him.

Before getting into his car, he stopped and took a deep breath of the cool night air. He felt as if he'd come from a very stuffy, very unpleasant place, and he knew he'd never be calling Gayle again.

He drove toward the foothills. The radio was turned up especially loud, as if to drown his thoughts. He didn't want to think about Caroline anymore that night. He intended to follow the plan, to wait a week before calling her again, so that she would be kept off balance, unsure of him and their relationship.

Besides, seeing her too often was dangerous for him. The more he was with her, the more he wanted to be with her. Slowly, in little ways, he felt himself opening up to her. She got to him.

No, he told himself again for about the tenth time that day, he couldn't let himself see her again too soon. He would wait....

And yet as he drove toward the foothills away from the city, he felt himself pulled back. Intensely vivid memories flashed through his mind—Caroline's smile, radiating warmth; Caroline's lips, soft and pliant; Caroline's body, fitting so perfectly with his, two parts of one whole.

Glancing at the clock on the dashboard, he saw that it was late, past eleven. Caroline was undoubtedly in bed, asleep. Which was exactly where Rafe would be in a matter of minutes.

The urgent feeling that had been building within him all evening intensified. He imagined Caroline lying there, alone, wearing some light summer nightgown...or, perhaps, wearing nothing at all.

Swearing under his breath, Rafe pulled the car to a halt in the middle of the deserted road. Then he turned it expertly and sped back toward Clovis.

The ringing of the doorbell roused Caroline from a fitful sleep. At first she thought she was dreaming. But the ringing continued and she realized someone really was at her front door. Looking at the bedside clock through blurred eyes, she saw that it was nearly midnight. Who on earth would come over at this hour? she wondered.

Throwing off the covers, she got out of bed, grabbed the white cotton robe that matched her nightgown and with tired, clumsy fingers tied the ribbons that laced up the front as she hurried to the door.

She looked through the window next to the door and was thoroughly startled to find Rafe standing there, his hands thrust in his pockets, his shirt unbuttoned and his tie askew.

As she threw open the door, stunned surprise and something more registered on her face.

"Rafe, what on earth—"

If she said anything more, he didn't hear it. He only knew that she managed to look at once innocent and seductive in her pristine white negligee with its lacy collar and nearly transparent thinness.

He pulled her against him roughly, crushing the thin cotton of the negligee beneath his chest. He kissed her then with all the pent-up desire of twenty-four long hours away from her. He meant to plunder her, to exorcise her magnetic attraction for him by taking her harshly.

Instead, the moment their lips met, the unreasonable anger he felt toward her was vanquished. In its place was passion of a pure intensity.

She melted in his arms, her lips yielding eagerly to his, and she offered no resistance. She didn't know why he'd come, especially so late. Nor why he seemed so angry. She only knew that he was there, holding her, and nothing else mattered.

Picking her up, he carried her to the bedroom, kicking the door shut behind him as he held her. Her arms were around his neck, her face buried against the smooth silk of his shirt.

As he laid her down on the bed, she whispered, once, "Rafe..."

As their eyes locked for one spellbound moment, Caroline felt the exquisite fusion of sensuality and emotion that only one man—this man—had ever elicited from her.

And she knew that he felt it, too.

Ignoring the row of ribbons tied in bows all down the front of the robe, he tore it off her. The gown followed. Caroline didn't protest as the thin cotton was ripped from her body. All she cared about at that moment was feeling his skin against hers.

His own clothes followed quickly. And then they were making love, wildly, with unbridled passion. There was nothing gentle about the kisses he rained over every part of her body. They were fierce, possessive, plundering. Her hunger for him was like a raging fire deep inside, an inferno that could be quenched in only one way.

He took her, filling her to her very depths. Gasping with joy, she reached up to wrap her hands around his neck and pull his mouth down to hers.

His hands were all over her, caressing, kneading, driving her wilder and wilder. Her fingers gripped his shoulders, her nails digging into his skin.

Both were panting and twisting, desperate to be part of each other. There was no sound in the room except their ragged breathing. But the pounding of their hearts sounded incredibly loud to each of them.

Then the ultimate explosion rocked both of them at once, and they trembled as they clasped each other tightly.

Slowly...slowly...Caroline came down to earth. Her mind cleared and her senses calmed. A sense of wonderment filled her at what she had just experienced. Even when they had made love the day before, it hadn't been like this. So intense that it was almost frightening.

Rafe still lay half on her, his head resting on her breasts as he took deep breaths to steady himself. Both his hands were still entwined with hers in a grip she couldn't hope to break.

He still hadn't said a word since drowning her own brief words in his searing kiss.

Bending down, Caroline gently kissed the top of his head. His dark hair felt soft and silky against her lips.

With womanly wisdom, she realized that he had needed her desperately. And, for some unknown reason, he'd wanted to resist that need. Giving in to it had cost him something. Perhaps it had cost both of them something. She wasn't sure. There was too much going on under the surface that she didn't understand.

The only thing she knew at that moment with absolute clarity was that she had needed him as well.

"Go to sleep," she whispered, with all the tenderness a mother might show to a very small child.

Then, finally unclasping one hand from his, she reached down and pulled the blanket over them. Closing her eyes, she immediately fell into a profound sleep.

Chapter Seven

Rafe left before Caroline awoke the next morning. He didn't call all day, but it didn't bother her. Somehow, she hadn't expected him to. However, shortly after she arrived home that evening, a delivery man arrived with a package. It was from a lingerie shop and when Caroline opened the box and drew aside the pale, peach-colored tissue, she found a lovely white negligee.

There was no note with it.

None was necessary.

On August fifteenth The Dollhouse opened. A small ad had appeared in the Home and Garden section of the local newspaper on the weekend before the opening. A banner across the window of the shop announced: Grand Opening. Inside, near the door, a small stand held a sign that read, *Please sign up for a draw to win this free doll*. The doll was a black-haired, blue-eyed baby dressed in a white lace christening gown and was one of Caroline's favorites.

On the counter was a small notice informing customers that dolls could be made-to-order in any style the customer wished. But the notice was barely visible behind the plants that well-wishers had sent. With bright red ribbons tied around the gold foil at their base, the plants added to the lovely decor of the shop. Both Caroline and Marcia had spent hours combing antique shops for old pictures with dolls in them. These pictures now covered the walls.

As she opened the door at precisely ten o'clock, Marcia turned to Caroline and said with a grin, "I feel like we should break a bottle of champagne over something."

"I know. Why don't we settle for drinking it, instead, on Friday after work?"

"Great idea. You know, Jill offered to come in and help if we get busy. We should take advantage of that, because next week she leaves for school."

"Okay. That was nice of her to offer to spend her last week of summer vacation helping us out."

"She's a nice kid, if I do say so myself. By the way, what are we going to do about lunch if we're really busy? We don't want to keep customers waiting on our very first day. That could give us a reputation for sloppy service."

Caroline's smile was tolerant. "Let's worry about the rush when and if it comes. At the moment, you and I are the only people in the place."

"That's because we've only been open five minutes. Just wait."

They waited all morning. But by noon, only three people had come in, and two of them were friends of

Marcia's who stopped by to wish them well. Both friends admired the dolls, but neither bought one.

Then in the early afternoon, the mailman came in. He was a short, middle-aged man with graying blond hair and the brightest blue eyes this side of Paul Newman. His rather attractive face was creased with what Caroline quickly decided must be a perennial smile.

"Hi, ladies. I see you're finally open."

Marcia gave him a rueful look. "You couldn't tell that by the business we're doing."

"Ah, don't worry. It's only your first day. Here's your mail. Besides all the stuff addressed to 'occupant' there's actually one with your name on it."

Glancing through the small pile of mail he handed her, Marcia said with a laugh, "Wouldn't you know?—it's a bill."

The mailman went on, "Maybe tomorrow I'll have something more welcome for you."

"Will you be coming at this same time every day?"

"Six days a week, rain or shine. By the way, my name's Jack Dinwiddie." Marcia and Caroline introduced themselves.

Jack, who was clearly a friendly sort, said, "You two ladies partners?"

They both nodded. Marcia added, "Caroline made these dolls by hand."

"They sure are nice. What gave you the idea to open up a shop?"

"We sort of found ourselves at a crossroads. I'm divorced and Marcia's widowed. We thought it would be exciting to have our own business."

Caroline finished ruefully, "Although it would be more exciting if we actually had some customers."

Jack smiled reassuringly. "You'll get customers. Don't worry. You've got some really nice things here. I know how popular dolls are. My wife used to collect 'em."

The look he gave Marcia was warm with compassion. "That was before she died. I'm a widower myself, y'see. Well, I'd better be going. See you tomorrow."

When he was gone, Marcia said, "I didn't realize how quiet it's been in here, until that conversation with him. It's pretty bad when the only person we have to talk to all day is the mailman."

"At least he's nice."

"Mmm, I guess so," Marcia replied disinterestedly.

In the late afternoon she left to run some errands, and Caroline was alone in the shop. Since business was so dismal, there was no question of calling Jill to ask her to help out.

Then a little girl of about eleven or twelve came in. She wasn't really a customer, but Caroline made a point of waiting on her as carefully as she would have done with a wealthy matron.

"May I help you, miss?" she asked politely.

The girl, who had carrot-red hair and freckles, seemed a little nervous. "Is it okay to look around?"

"Of course."

"I won't break anything."

Caroline smiled. "I'm sure you won't. Do you know about porcelain dolls?"

The girl shook her head. "But they looked so pretty from outside. Especially that baby doll," she finished, pointing to the doll that was to be the prize in the free drawing.

Caroline explained at length how the dolls were made and let the girl hold the baby doll.

"Gosh, I've never seen anything like this before. I've got a doll but she's made out of rubber. And she sure doesn't look this pretty."

"This is the way really nice dolls used to be made. This one is a copy of a baby doll that was made over a hundred years ago."

The girl's green eyes grew round with wonder. "No kidding? A hundred years?"

Caroline nodded.

"You mean all that time ago some girl just like me maybe was playing with a doll that looked just like this?"

"That's right."

"How neat."

Then, hesitating a little, she asked, "How much does this one cost?"

"That one is the prize in a drawing we're having today. But I can make another exactly like it. The price is four hundred and fifty dollars."

The figure obviously floored the girl. Reluctantly, she handed the doll back to Caroline as if afraid she might break it and have to pay for it. But the look in her eyes was so filled with longing, that Caroline knew she'd fallen in love with the doll.

Taking in the girl's faded T-shirt and cheap jeans, she asked casually, "Do you live around here?"

"No. My mom cleans a house near here. She brought me with her today 'cause I'm out of school. But I got bored and she said I could look around this shopping center."

"I'm glad you came in. I hope you'll stop by again sometime."

"Okay. Well, I guess I'd better go."

She gave the baby doll one last lingering look that was utterly poignant in its hopelessness.

Suddenly Caroline had an idea. "Before you go, why don't you fill out one of these slips for our draw. I was just getting ready to hold it. Who knows, you might win."

"You think so?"

"Sure. You've got as much chance as anyone."

The girl took a pen from Caroline and carefully wrote her name and address on the slip of paper.

Taking it from her, Caroline read, "Cindy Cox. What a pretty name. Maybe it will be a lucky one."

She dropped the slip in the narrow slit on the top of a small box. She made a point of shaking the box vigorously, apparently to mix up the slips inside. All the while, Cindy watched anxiously.

Then, taking the top off the box, Caroline closed her eyes and reached inside, pulling out one slip. Opening her eyes, she read, "Cindy Cox. What do you know?—you won!" Unobtrusively she dropped the slip back into the box.

Cindy's mouth fell open with surprise. "I really did?"

Caroline laughed. "You really did. Here, let me wrap up the doll for you."

As she put it in tissue paper, then laid it carefully in a box, she went on, "It's very fragile, you know, Cindy. You will take care of it, won't you?"

"Oh, yes, ma'am. Oh, *yes*. I'll put it up on my dresser and I won't let anyone else touch it, unless I make sure their hands are clean. Oh, I've never had anything like this before! Wait till my mom sees it."

"Here's a receipt in case your mom has any questions about where you got it."

Cindy took the receipt and stuffed it in her jeans pocket. Then she left, carrying the doll as carefully as if it were a real live baby.

As she walked out the door, Rafe held it open for her.

Seeing him, Caroline felt surprise, then pleasure. She hadn't realized he had been standing there.

Walking up to her, he asked, "Whose name was really on that paper?"

She smiled innocently. "What do you mean?"

"I mean that was a rigged draw if ever I saw one."

She sighed. "Well, there were only half a dozen slips in there. And all the others were women who could easily afford to buy a doll."

"I thought the whole point of the draw was free publicity? Somehow, I doubt that any of Cindy's friends will see her doll, then come in here to buy one for themselves."

"Maybe not. But, oh, Rafe, did you see how badly she wanted it? Haven't you ever wanted something that badly, something unattainable?"

His teasing expression slowly faded and he was silent for a moment. Finally, he said slowly, "Yes...I've wanted something that badly. Something unattainable."

He was looking at her in a way he'd never done before. His gray eyes were open, unguarded, and what Caroline saw in them took her breath away.

He's going to say "I love you," she thought. The idea was both frightening and exhilarating.

Silently they looked at one another, and it was a moment suspended in time. Rafe opened his mouth to speak, and Caroline stealed herself for what must come.

Then Marcia's voice shattered the intimacy of the moment. "Rafe, what a nice surprise!"

In an instant his expression changed utterly.

With a sinking sensation, Caroline realized that the moment was lost.

As Marcia walked around behind the counter, she asked, "Did we have any more customers?"

"No... not exactly. But since it's so close to closing time, I went ahead and had the drawing. A little girl who was in the shop won."

"A little girl? That's nice. I hope all her friends are green with envy and persuade their mothers to buy them a doll, too."

Somehow, Caroline didn't have the heart to tell Marcia that this particular little girl didn't look like she had rich friends. She was relieved when Rafe didn't comment on the fact, either.

He said easily, "I take it you're having a slow opening."

Marcia grimaced. "Yes, darn it. There can't have been more than ten people in here all day."

"Well, don't get discouraged. It's just your first day. You'll get more customers once people start hearing about you."

"Do you really think so?" Caroline asked. She hated the vaguely desperate note in her voice, but she couldn't help it. The day had begun with such high hopes, and it was ending so dismally.

"I really think so," Rafe responded with a reassuring smile. "Besides, it's the middle of August, and a lot of people are away on vacation. By September, when everyone's back in town, and you're better known, you'll be doing great."

Marcia forced a confident smile. "I'll bet you're right. Now if you two will excuse me, I'm gonna take these supplies into our office. And I use the term loosely."

She disappeared into the tiny back room that was crammed full of boxes, tissue paper, doll supplies and one small, battered desk that had previously been in her son, Jason's bedroom.

Turning back to Rafe, Caroline asked, "Want to come over for dinner tonight?"

"I've got a better idea. I'll take you out. You probably don't really feel like cooking."

"Oh, I don't mind. It's good therapy, actually. But it's nice of you to offer to take me out."

"We'll go some place very special and I'll spend the entire evening cheering you up."

"Don't get the wrong idea. Marcia and I are both disappointed that people aren't beating a path to our door. But we really weren't expecting to be an overnight success."

"That's wise. Any business takes awhile to get off the ground. Speaking of business, I've got to get over to a ground breaking ceremony for a new shopping center. I'll pick you up about eight, if that sounds okay."

"Sounds great. See you then."

As he left, Caroline felt a lingering wistfulness. They had come close to something a few minutes earlier before Marcia had arrived. Part of her hoped they could recapture the closeness later. But part of her was afraid. Despite what she'd told Marcia about putting the past behind her, that was much easier said than done. Every time she felt herself growing close to Rafe, she remembered how deeply he had hurt her once. The bitter memory put a subtle but unmistakable distance between them, as surely as if a wall went up separating them.

That evening Caroline relaxed in a hot bath in her lavender and mint-green bathroom. She'd spruced up the old bathroom with paint and hanging plants, which thrived in the moist air. And though the white tile was chipped, and the fixtures were old, the bathroom was actually quite pleasant.

She lazed in the warm water for several minutes, thinking about her first day in business. It certainly hadn't turned out the way she had imagined, but she refused to let herself panic yet. As both Rafe and the friendly mailman, Jack, had said, it was just the first day. It took awhile for any business to get off the ground.

Deep inside, Caroline had a feeling of déjà vu. She'd been there before, in a way. When Marina was born, and Caroline left the hospital with her, she had felt frightened but determined. Somehow, she knew, she would make everything work out. She had to. There was no alternative, for Marina's happiness and welfare were at stake.

Now she felt the same way. Somehow she would make this business work out. There was no alternative, because this time her own welfare was at stake.

When the water turned tepid, Caroline stepped out of the tub. As she dried off with a huge lavender bath sheet and slipped on a short white terry cloth robe, the shop was no longer on her mind. Rafe was. Soon she would see him. And before the evening was over, they would make love. The very thought made her spine tingle with anticipation.

As she dabbed her most expensive perfume behind her ears, at the base of her throat and behind her knees, she knew that these places would soon feel Rafe's touch and kiss.

She spent an hour getting her hair and makeup absolutely perfect. Finally, she put on real silk stockings, silver sandals with high, spike heels and her favorite dressy dress made of turquoise silk, sleeveless, knee length, with a plunging neckline that didn't allow for a bra.

Rafe had said he was taking her some place very special, and she wanted to look her very best. She was just putting turquoise studs in her ears, when Rafe arrived.

He whistled appreciatively, and she smiled with delight.

"You look marvelous."

"Thank you. You look pretty marvelous yourself."

He wore a light-tan blazer over a white silk shirt that was unbuttoned at the neck just enough to reveal wisps of dark, curling chest hair. The matching tan slacks fit just tight enough to emphasize Rafe's slim hips and sinewy thighs.

He looked so devastatingly sexy that Caroline's mind was immediately filled with highly erotic thoughts. These made her blush furiously.

"Something wrong?" Rafe asked, looking at her intently.

"No...I...no," she stammered, then felt like kicking herself for being so silly. But she couldn't help it. The man brought out her deepest sexuality.

"Hungry?" he asked as they walked out to his car.

"Starved. I didn't have lunch today."

"Neither did I."

"Were you terribly busy?" she asked as he opened the car door for her.

He nodded. "It was one of those days when everything seemed to go wrong. We're behind schedule on one project, and another one that we were preparing to start soon was scuttled by the Planning Commission. Actually, I can't blame them. It was for an apartment complex here in Clovis, and there are getting to be too many of those now. Our complex was going to be a lot better than the average, but we couldn't convince the commission of that."

"When you say 'we' does that mean you work with someone?"

He looked surprised. "Haven't I mentioned my partner, Jim Hansen?"

"No." Caroline didn't add that he had told her almost nothing of his business, or his personal life, for that matter.

"He's an architect, the creative half of the team. I handle the financial end."

"Sounds like a perfect partnership."

"It is, actually. Jim's very easy to work with."

She couldn't resist responding, "Unlike you."

Rafe flashed her a startled look, then laughed good-naturedly. "You're right. Unlike me. When something goes wrong, I want to put my fist through a wall. Jim just shrugs and figures out a way to go around the obstruction."

"Has he been a mellowing influence on you?" Caroline asked with a teasing smile.

"Well . . . I haven't put my fist through a wall in quite a while."

"Do you like your work, Rafe?"

The question seemed to catch him off guard. "I suppose so. I never really think of it in terms of enjoyment. It's an interesting challenge. And I like challenges."

That she could easily believe. When he was younger, he had certainly challenged the smug assumptions of the social order, rather than accepting them as his very traditional father had done.

Thinking of his father reminded Caroline that she'd meant to ask about his parents. She hadn't done so yet because they were part of the past. And everything about the past was verboten. But she was genuinely curious about his parents. Though she'd never met his mother, she had known his father, who had come to her parents' house once a week to do the gardening. He was a nice, kind man, who worked incredibly hard, quietly accepted his position at the bottom of Clovis society and doted on his wife and child.

Looking at Rafe now in the dark quiet of the car, she said, "Your parents must be very proud of your success."

Immediately the atmosphere in the car changed perceptibly. There was a tense silence, and she sensed that it had been the wrong thing to say.

Finally, Rafe answered without looking at her. "They were. They're dead now."

"I'm sorry to hear that. Your father was a wonderful person. I didn't know your mother, but your father always spoke so lovingly of her, I'm sure she must have been very nice, too."

Rafe's mouth was set in a tight line and he kept his eyes glued to the road. "She was. She worked damned hard so they could afford to give me the same things more well-to-do kids had. Clothes and things. It meant a lot to her that I didn't feel inferior in any way."

Caroline had no idea how to respond to that. What could she say, she wondered, that wouldn't sound condescending or insincere?

The tense silence between them stretched out for several minutes while Caroline tried desperately to think of something to say.

Finally, Rafe said, "Let's change the subject, shall we?"

Feeling wretched, Caroline nodded. They'd been happy and at ease with each other only moments earlier.

Now the atmosphere between them was strained. All because she had brought up one seemingly innocent subject from the past. It was a hard lesson she wouldn't forget. If she and Rafe were to continue to have any kind of relationship, it had to start with the present, as if they'd never known each other before.

She had to tell herself that they were two people meeting for the first time, not two people who had first met, and first loved, years ago. That wouldn't be an easy trick to bring off, she realized. The only way to do it was to concentrate totally on the here and now.

"Tell me about your company, what you've built," she urged, trying to make her voice sound as normal as possible.

To her relief, Rafe seemed more than happy to talk about his company.

"The first thing we did was to convert an old house in the Tower District into a lawyer's office. We had so little money back then that I worked along with the construction crew. Even now, I still like to put on a hard hat and get up on a half-finished building. There's an exhilaration there you don't get sitting behind a desk."

Caroline grimaced. "I'm terrified of heights. I don't know how construction workers do it, walking around on a narrow board several stories off the ground. They must have the sense of balance of ballet dancers."

Rafe's lips curved softly in a half-smile. It was the first sign of a real thaw in the coolness that had sprung up between them, and Caroline felt a rush of relief.

"That's the first time I've heard construction workers compared to ballet dancers. But actually I think you're right."

"Do you do housing developments?"

"No. Commercial real estate's safer. There's not as much fluctuation in the market. And there's more money there."

Money. Always money. Caroline wondered if it had brought Rafe happiness, but she didn't dare ask.

Gradually she noticed that they were heading out of town toward the foothills.

"Are we going to the Pheasant Run?"

Rafe shook his head, and a look of sly amusement came into his gray eyes.

She went on, "We're not by any chance going all the way up to Yosemite Park to the Ahwahnee Restaurant?"

"Nope. This place is much closer than that. In fact, we're just about there."

Looking around, Caroline saw nothing but grape vineyards stretching up to the foothills, interspersed with occasional houses.

"I didn't know there was a restaurant around here," she commented curiously.

Rafe's smile broadened. "Oh, this place is very exclusive."

After a few more minutes, he turned off the highway onto a smaller road that climbed up a low hill. In the darkness, Caroline couldn't make out any of their surroundings. But as they climbed higher, she saw the glittering lights of Clovis and Fresno in the distance.

Then the car topped the brow of the hill and they came out onto a broad, circular drive in front of a brightly lit house.

Caroline realized instinctively that this was Rafe's home. Somehow, it was exactly as she would have expected it to be. New. Modern. Stunning. Built of white stucco, it was two stories tall, with huge windows looking out over the valley below.

Smiling wryly at Rafe, she said, "Exclusive, huh?"

He stopped the car. As he got out, then opened the door for her, he responded, "Very exclusive. You and I will be the only diners here."

In the three weeks she had been involved with Rafe, he hadn't once brought her to his home. Caroline sensed that this was an important moment. He was opening up to her, sharing more of his personal life. She felt very touched, and very happy.

And yet as they went inside, she couldn't find it within herself to like his house. It was absolutely magnificent, a work of architectural daring. And the decor was impressive, like something out of *Architectural Digest*. Bold modern art covered the white walls, and the furniture was soft, cream-colored leather. It was as if someone with a great deal of money had given a high priced decorator carte blanche.

Which, Caroline realized, is probably exactly what had happened.

Stunning as it was, it was a showplace, not a home. There was no warmth, and no sense of individuality.

Rafe didn't ask what she thought of his home, but Caroline felt good manners required her to say something. Walking over to the huge, floor to ceiling window that took up most of one wall of the living room, she looked out.

"You've got a fabulous view of the valley."

"Yes. That's why I chose this site to build on. Would you like a drink before dinner?"

"No thanks. What are we having for dinner?"

"Mushroom quiche, salad and pilaf."

"Mmm, sounds delicious. Don't tell me you cooked it."

He smiled. "No. I can barely boil water. My housekeeper made dinner and left it in the oven on warm. I thought we'd eat out on the patio."

"It's a lovely night for it, not too hot."

He led her out through sliding glass doors to a stone patio that ran along the entire back of the house. On the patio, a small table was set with white linen and pristine white china.

He lit the tall white candle in the center of the table, then said, "I'll be right back."

Caroline nodded. As Rafe went inside, he flicked a switch, and the outside light went out, leaving the area lit by soft candlelight.

Caroline walked over to the waist-high wall that ran along the patio and looked out at the valley. There was a full moon illuminating the landscape. Shadows of charcoal-gray and black moved as wispy clouds slid past the moon, obscuring it for a moment, then moving on.

It was a cool night for mid-August, and a light breeze stirred the leaves of the small potted trees on the broad patio. Closing her eyes, Caroline breathed in the fresh, clean country air. Somewhere in the distance an owl called forlornly, then stopped, and all was silent.

Behind her, Rafe set a tray holding their dinner down on the table. Uncorking a bottle of white wine, he put it in a silver wine cooler. Then he looked over at Caroline standing quietly in the moonlight. Her hair, which hung loose as he preferred it, was the palest silvery-blond in the moonlight. The thin silk of her dress clung to her slender figure, outlining the gentle swell of her hips and the round thrust of her breasts.

Walking over to her, he wrapped his arms around her waist and buried his face in her hair. It smelled sweet and clean. As his head bent further to kiss her earlobe, the subtle, seductive scent of her perfume filled his senses.

At the same time, his arms wrapped more tightly around her and moved upward. The instant he touched the soft swell of her breasts and realized they were unconstrained, he felt an intense tightening deep in his abdomen.

Pulling back, he quickly undid the zipper in the back of her dress just enough to slip his hands inside. Reaching around, he cupped her breasts. Caroline gasped, then arched against him, turning her head just enough so that he could nuzzle her cheek.

As his fingers gently kneaded her breasts, his mouth moved down her cheek, her throat, to her shoulder, where the dress had slipped off it, raining kisses on her satiny skin.

Both were on fire now, their breath coming faster, their bodies trembling.

Turning her to face him, Rafe pulled her into a tight embrace and kissed her long and hard. When the kiss finally ended, Caroline opened her eyes to stare into his. Naked desire shone in their golden depths.

Suddenly Rafe picked her up and started to carry her inside.

Her face was wreathed in smiles as she said teasingly, "But dinner..."

"To hell with dinner!" he snapped.

He strode to his bedroom. Without pausing to turn on the light, he laid her on his bed. Then, with every ounce of patience he could muster, he carefully undressed her, taking infinite care with the silk dress.

When she lay naked before him, he threw off his jacket. Then, as he started to unbutton his shirt, Caroline said, "Here... let me."

Reaching up, she undid the buttons one by one, with excruciating slowness. As each button was undone, she tenderly kissed the patch of skin that was revealed. When his shirt was off, she began to slowly unbuckle his belt.

"You're driving me crazy," he whispered hoarsely.

She smiled up at him. "Patience is a virtue, you know."

"Well, it's a virtue I don't have."

In an instant he was out of the remainder of his clothes and pressing his hard body along the length of her soft one. And after that, neither felt like wasting time with talk.

Chapter Eight

Late that night, Rafe and Caroline, dressed only in robes, finally returned to the patio to eat the dinner they'd left there hours earlier. But as they reached the sliding glass doors, they saw the food lying on the ground and a raccoon picking through the quiche, rice and salad.

Putting a finger to her lips, Caroline motioned to Rafe to be quiet. Standing there, they watched as the little gray marauder, with his black mask, enjoyed their dinner. He was quite well-mannered about it, licking his claws when they seemed to get dirty and eating only a little at a time. He had already gotten through most of the food, and it only took a few minutes for him to finish.

"Do you think we should ask if he'd like dessert?" Caroline whispered as he finished.

"No, he's made a pig of himself. Besides, uninvited guests can't expect too much."

Suddenly sensing their presence, the raccoon looked up, his dark eyes fearful. For a moment he stared at the humans, then turned and scurried away.

"Well, so much for dinner," Rafe said lightly. "I hope the little rascal appreciated Maria's cooking."

"It certainly looked like he did. I can scramble some eggs for us, if you'd like."

"Okay. I'm starved."

Caroline smiled shyly. "So am I."

In his kitchen, Rafe made toast while Caroline scrambled eggs, shallots and herbs. Then, putting it on two trays, along with a bottle of wine, they returned to his bedroom.

Sitting on his rumpled bed, they ate the simple but delicious meal. Neither cared that it was scrambled eggs rather than the gourmet meal Maria had prepared.

When they'd finished, Rafe looked at Caroline and said with a seductive glint in his pale eyes, "You do wonders for that robe."

Quickly, she darted a glance at the chocolate-brown velour robe that would have come to Rafe's knees but fell in heavy folds nearly to her ankles. Then, smiling at him, she responded, "It's comfortable. Eating in bed is comfortable, too. But somehow this wasn't how I expected to be having dinner."

"Disappointed?"

She shook her head slowly. "No, definitely not disappointed."

Putting his tray on a bedside table, Rafe picked up his half-full wine glass and slowly sipped the dry white wine. He leaned against the pillows piled at the headboard of his bed, and for a moment he watched Caroline as she finished the last of her wine. Her hair was in sexy disarray, and her pale skin was still slightly flushed from their ardent lovemaking. Realizing that he could affect her so profoundly made him feel powerful—and rather tender somehow.

Then he noticed the deep V-neck of the robe hanging open just enough to reveal her small, firm breasts, and he felt a vague stirring in his loins. Before this night was over, that stirring would be a great deal more than vague, he knew. They would make love again, and when they did, he knew that she would respond with the same uninhibited passion as always. Her response fired his own passion and made him even more ardent.

And yet he knew that despite the way that she had opened up to him physically, she hadn't entirely opened up emotionally. She was holding back, protecting her heart. She hadn't said, "I love you," and didn't seem to want him to say those words to her. And while he sensed sometimes that she wanted to open up to him, to communicate about intimate subjects rather than their usual impersonal conversation, she always pulled back.

If he was going to make her fall in love with him, he knew it was time he got to know her on another level besides the physical one.

"Tell me about your marriage."

The abrupt question caught Caroline off guard. She shot a startled glance at Rafe, then looked down at her wine, making a pretense of being very interested in it.

Ignoring the question, she said, "This is marvelous wine. What is it?"

"Caroline, I asked you a question."

"A very personal question."

"Yes."

The awkward silence stretched out for seconds, then minutes. Finally, Rafe repeated, "Tell me about your marriage."

"I don't want to talk about it."

The flat refusal took him by surprise. She was, indeed, stronger then the shy, fragile seventeen-year-old girl he'd once been able to dominate.

Changing his tone, he went on less brusquely, "I need to know."

She looked at him with big, round, haunted eyes. "Why do you need to know? It has nothing to do with you."

"Yes it does. Because it has to do with you. I don't know very much about you, really."

"Then we're even, because I know almost nothing about you except that you're fiercely ambitious."

"Maybe it's time we got to know each other outside of bed."

The suggestion clearly wasn't one she was expecting. The expression in her eyes revealed that she was torn between reluctance to open up and a desire for a greater closeness with him. Holding his breath, he waited for her to choose.

Looking away from him, she said slowly, "His name is Edward Turner. I was twenty when we got married. We were divorced a few months ago."

It was the barest statement of facts, leaving out all the emotion that must have been involved in a marriage that had lasted for more than twenty years. But it was a beginning.

"Why did you marry him?"

She met his look. "People usually get married because they've fallen in love."

It was unlike her to make a remark that was meant to wound, as that one clearly was meant to wound him. It suggested that this was a very sensitive subject for her, which only made Rafe all the more determined to learn all about it.

"I don't think you were in love with him. Why did you marry him?"

For a moment it looked as if she might simply get angry and refuse to talk any further. Then, her lips curved in a barely perceptible smile.

"It's rather vain of you to believe I never loved anyone else."

He met her look. "I know you never loved anyone else. Vanity has nothing to do with it."

"How can you be so damned sure about that?" she asked angrily.

"Because you couldn't possibly have loved a man who was obviously a sexual cretin."

She stopped, speechless. He could see her anger slowly fading, and knew the shot he'd taken was an accurate one.

He repeated in a tone that was infinitely patient, "So why did you marry him?"

Without hesitation, she answered glibly, "People said we made a perfect couple, both blond and brown-eyed. We looked right together."

"That's why you got married?"

"In a way."

That was far from being the whole truth, he knew. He waited for her to continue. When she didn't, he pressed, "Why did you really marry him?"

Frustration and defensiveness were etched in her face. "Don't you ever give up?"

"If I did I'd be a gardener like my father. Answer the question." As an afterthought, he added with surprising gentleness, "Please."

She looked at him long and hard. Finally, she answered slowly, "It seemed like the right thing to do at the time." Meeting his look of disbelief, she finished, "That's the truth, Rafe. You may not find it a satisfactory answer, but it's the only one I have."

He still didn't believe that he had gotten the whole truth from her, but he sensed that she wouldn't reveal anything more. Changing the subject, he went on, "Why did you get a divorce?"

Strangely enough, she didn't seem so reluctant to discuss this. She answered easily, "He was a successful businessman. Like you, it mattered to him to have a nice house, drive an impressive car and belong to the most exclusive country club."

"I don't belong to a country club."

She smiled. "That's because you despise the people who do."

He met her smile. "That's true. Still, it must have been a comfortable life for you."

"Oh, yes, it was definitely comfortable. A full-time housekeeper, vacations in the Caribbean, shopping at Neiman-Marcus and Saks. Everything most women think will make them happy and content."

"But you weren't. Happy and content, that is."

She shook her head and a wisp of straight blond hair lay across her cheek. Reaching over, Rafe tenderly brushed it aside. His touch made her stop and give him a startled look.

"Why didn't you work?" he asked.

Her dry smile returned. "It just wasn't done. This was still the nineteen sixties, remember. Women weren't going into the work force in droves then. I was supposed to stay home and be a perfect hostess and do volunteer work for charities. All of which I did."

"And in your spare time you made dolls?"

"Yes. I never thought of it as a way to make real money. It was just a hobby to fill my time. Edward spent a lot of time at work, and I was alone quite a bit. I loved making dolls and discovered that I had a talent for it, which was odd since I didn't particularly show any artistic talent in school. Then Marcia suggested we open up the shop. At first I thought she was crazy or at least unrealistic. Then I realized that experts always say if you're going to have a business it should involve what you do best. Making dolls is my one and only talent."

But it wasn't really her business that Rafe was interested in. "Did you want the divorce or did he?" he asked bluntly.

She met his look without flinching, and at that instant he felt profound admiration for her. Whatever else he might feel about her, he had to admit she had courage.

"Edward wanted the divorce. His business failed, you see, which was a great deal more traumatic for him than it was for me. I'd gotten to the point where I didn't really care for that big, empty house. And a person can only do so much shopping before it becomes redundant. But Edward was shattered. He didn't know who he was if he wasn't a successful businessman. He found someone else to comfort him and make him feel less like a failure."

Rafe felt a surge of anger toward Edward Turner. It wasn't the first time he had felt it. Beating it down, he went on ruthlessly, "That must have hurt."

To his surprise, there was absolutely no trace of bitterness in her tone as she responded, "Well, my ego was bruised, of course. To be forty-two and replaced by a younger woman is, I think, every wife's nightmare. But once I got over the initial rejection, I wasn't really hurt. Not really. Edward had been very good to . . . to me for a long time. And if his entire world hadn't crumbled around him, I think he would have continued being good. Of course, there was some humiliation because everyone else seemed to know about his affair before I did.''

Humiliation was something Rafe understood all too well. Just thinking about it touched that cold, hard place at his very core where his heart had once been. The coldness, the hardness, had been forged by humiliation. And that humiliation had to do with Caroline.

The tenderness he'd begun to feel toward her dissolved and he went on curtly, "So you came back to Clovis because your life in San Francisco had fallen apart.''

She didn't seem to resent the harsh way he'd phrased it. Her expression was completely calm as she answered, ''Yes.''

There was no self-pity in her tone, or even fear. She was facing a difficult situation with honesty and courage.

''Even though it had been a long time since I left here, it still felt like home,'' she went on.

Remembering why she left, he felt all pity for her slowly fade. Even though she was having a hard time now, obviously she'd had it made for quite a while. The loss that had eaten away at him every day of his life didn't seem to have had any effect on her.

Without saying a word, he picked up both their trays and took them into the kitchen. When he returned, he found her curled up against the pillows at the head of the bed, watching him with a hurt, puzzled expression. He knew what she was thinking. She had opened up to him, and now, for some reason, there was a distance between them again.

Ignoring her hurt look, he said, "I'm glad you told me. I understand your situation better now."

"What about you?"

Immediately he was on his guard. "What do you mean?"

"Why didn't you ever marry?"

"I think I answered that question once."

"Not really. Saying that you're a confirmed bachelor doesn't explain why you feel that way."

"Maybe I haven't seen enough happy marriages to convince me the odds would be on my side."

"Funny, I thought you were the kind of man who wouldn't count the odds."

For an instant, he felt surprised at the unexpectedly perceptive thrust. Then he laughed easily. "You're right."

She smiled. "So why hasn't some calculating female gotten you to the altar?"

"It's flattering that you would think someone would try."

"Don't be coy. It doesn't suit you. You're very attractive, as you seem to know quite well, and what's even more important to most women, you're wealthy. I'm sure half the available women in town must be after you."

"How pleasant for me if you're right."

"Rafe! Beating around the bush with you is irritating. I gave you some straight answers. Can't you give me one?"

The only straight answer he could give her—that he'd never married because he'd never stopped loving her—was out of the question. Instead he gave a diluted version of the truth.

"I've never fallen in love, and as you pointed out, that's the usual reason for marriage."

She looked at him thoughtfully. He could see she didn't entirely buy that answer but she wasn't at all sure how to respond to it.

"Tell me about the boys' shelter you started."

The question was completely unexpected. It was also a subject he didn't like to discuss because comments on his altruism always made him feel embarrassed somehow.

"Where did you hear about that?"

"From Marcia."

"Of course. I should have known. I don't publicize my involvement with it."

"Why not? It's certainly an accomplishment to be proud of."

He didn't know how to explain his feelings to her, and he didn't want to. He had intended to explore her feelings tonight, not his.

"It's just a place where teenage boys can go when things get too rough for them at home. There's a counselor there." He shrugged. "It's not that big a deal." He tried to sound offhand but knew that he failed.

The look she gave him held real warmth. "Okay. I think I can understand why you don't want to talk about it."

"Do you?"

She nodded.

And suddenly he knew that she did understand. It rattled his composure to think that she could get inside him that way.

It was time, he decided, to change the subject.

"Want to go skinny-dipping?"

She grinned. "Skinny-dipping? Do you have a pool?"

"No. Unfortunately the configuration of this hill couldn't allow for one. But I have the next best thing. Come on, I'll show you."

He led her into what she had assumed was the bathroom from the limited view she'd gotten through the half-open door. But as they stepped inside and he turned on the light, she discovered that it was unlike any bathroom she'd been in before.

It was huge, at least as big as his bedroom, and that was a very good size. Shiny terra-cotta tile covered the floor, and the cabinets built into one wall were made of redwood. Along another wall an atrium area held lush plants that were nearly as tall as the ceiling. A shower made of clear glass was on one side of the atrium, and a large sunken tub was on the other.

But the focus of the room was a large round Jacuzzi that looked like a small swimming pool. Tiled steps led up to it and ferns trailed their deep emerald fronds just above the water level.

"Rafe, it's fabulous!"

"It's my favorite room in the house. When I'm uptight about something I can always relax in here."

"I can see why."

Rafe slipped off his robe, then took off Caroline's, letting it drop to the floor in a crumpled heap beside his own. As they stepped into the Jacuzzi together, Rafe pushed a button in a small console next to the Jacuzzi, and the water began to froth and bubble. It was warm, but not too warm, and Caroline immediately felt herself relax.

A narrow bench ran around the entire Jacuzzi. Rafe and Caroline sat at opposite sides, facing each other. As she leaned back, he pointed to the ceiling and said, "Look up."

When she did so, she saw that the entire ceiling above the Jacuzzi was a skylight. Stars shone brightly and the moon itself was just barely visible off to one side. Rafe pushed another button in the small console, and the skylight opened. At the same time, the lights in the room went out.

He and Caroline sat there in the darkness, with the stars shining above them and the water swirling around them. Through the open skylight, night sounds floated in—a cricket, the rustle of leaves in the wind. The cool night air felt refreshing on their upturned faces, as their bodies lounged in the warmth of the water.

Neither spoke. It was a time for silent contemplation, not mindless small talk. Caroline leaned her head back and closed her eyes.

Rafe watched the water eddy and flow around her. The water level was just below her breasts. As drops splashed on her, tiny beads trickled down the high, firm mounds. It was a highly erotic sight, and yet he didn't feel the desire to make love to her right then. He had no urge to do anything other than what he was doing—sitting there, watching Caroline, her face lit by moonlight.

He had shared this experience with other women, yet something was different about this night. Finally, he realized what it was. He was at peace. For the first time since he'd moved into the house, he didn't feel that something, some vague, nameless thing, was missing. Everything was complete.

He knew that it was because of Caroline. Her presence filled the emptiness of the big, lonely house and made it feel like a home. Once she was gone, it would never feel that way again.

He knew that he would never be able to sit in the Jacuzzi with another woman without remembering this night with Caroline. He would never be able to lie down in his bed again without remembering how she'd looked sitting there in his robe. He'd never be able to walk out onto his patio without remembering the sheer delight that had shone in her golden eyes as she'd watched the raccoon eat their dinner.

And no matter how many other women he made love to, he would always remember making love to this one.

He hadn't walked away from her yet, but already he felt a profound sense of loss. It had been a mistake to bring her here, he realized. Because this house would never be the same again without her.

At that moment she opened her eyes, and her gaze locked with his.

A flash of desire so intense it was like electricity arced between them. Without saying a word, Caroline swam over to him. As he sat there, arms outstretched on the rim of the Jacuzzi, she began to kiss his wet skin, licking the beads of water.

The feel of her lips, her tongue was almost unbearably sensuous as her mouth roved across his broad chest and hard, muscled shoulders. Her fingertips played in the damply curling tendrils of hair on his chest, then moved down beneath the water to his hips.

Rafe groaned low in his throat as Caroline's mouth moved lower and lower on his chest. Then, in a movement so swift it caught him entirely by surprise, she ducked her head under the water for one quick, unbelievably erotic kiss low on the flat plane of his stomach.

When her head came up, her hair hanging smooth and sleek and dripping wet, she was grinning mischievously. But he wiped the grin off her face by pulling her against him roughly and kissing her deeply. Her breasts pressed against his chest, her hips against his hips.

Like fire licking at a powder keg, the feel of her body on top of his made his passion explosive. His need to take her was urgent. It had been less than five minutes since he had sat there, feeling sated and at peace. But it might as well have been a lifetime ago, the way his body was on fire at that moment.

Putting his hands on her hips, he maneuvered her over him, and in a moment they were moving together in the warm, bubbling water. Her arms were around his neck; his were around her narrow waist. Their kisses grew frenzied, as they moved faster and faster together, until finally they couldn't go any faster and they spun out of control, out of consciousness, before coming to a shuddering, convulsive stop together....

Caroline clung to him, her face buried against his damp chest. Both were gasping for breath, exhausted, utterly sated as they had never been before.

As Rafe's mind cleared and he was once more capable of coherent thought, he wondered if it would always be like this with her—better and better each time. Impossible as it seemed, he felt it would be.

He brushed her wet hair back from her face, and as he did so, she looked up at him. He wasn't aware of how tender and loving the smile was that he gave her. Her own in response was shy yet unembarrassed. There was something almost exultant about her. Belatedly he realized that she was quite simply pleased with herself, with her unabashed behavior.

"You're a constant surprise, you know that?" he said in a husky voice.

"A pleasant surprise?" Her smile was teasing, yet he suspected she needed reassuring that her wantonness was seductive and not demeaning.

"Thoroughly pleasant."

I love you, Caroline.

The thought was so forceful that for a moment he was afraid he'd actually spoken out loud. The words felt so right, it was hard not to let them out.

Instead, he forced them down and said jokingly, "I'm not sure I can handle it. I'm not as young as I used to be."

She laughed softly. "Oh, I think you can handle it, Rafe. I suspect you can handle anything."

"Well, let's see if you're right."

Reaching over, he pushed the buttons that closed the skylight, turned on the lights, and turned off the Jacuzzi. Then he stood up abruptly, bringing her with him. Picking her up, he stepped out of the water and carried her over to a towel rack. He set her down, took a reddish-brown bath sheet off the rack and wrapped her in it.

Taking another, smaller towel off the rack, he began drying her hair, rubbing brusquely.

She laughed, and in the sound was all the innocent delight of a child at bath time. When he finally stopped drying her hair, she looked up at him through the damp tendrils and said in a husky, intimate voice, "I've never been like that before."

He stared into her eyes. "I know."

He knew that she wanted him to say that he hadn't either. And the truth was he hadn't. No other woman he'd known, even Gayle, who was thoroughly uninhibited, had ever made an experience more erotic.

Yet he held back, for the same reason he hadn't said "I love you" when he'd felt so much like saying it.

Instead, he said in a matter-of-fact tone, "I'd better get you home. You're a shopkeeper now and have to go to work tomorrow—or today, I should say, since it's after midnight."

He felt her intense disappointment, and for an instant it was almost as if the pain were his.

Then she pulled herself together and said in a voice that feigned casualness, "Of course. I shouldn't have stayed so late. I'll be exhausted in the morning."

Keeping the towel wrapped around her like a security blanket, she went into his bedroom. By the time he had dried off and joined her, she was dressed and was just pulling a comb through her tangled hair. As he dressed, she made a point of not looking at him.

Throughout the drive back to her house, she was silent. When he walked her to her door, she turned to face him.

"Thank you for a very special evening, Rafe. I'll never forget it. Ever. You've no idea what it means to me to discover that I can feel so much. I was afraid I would never feel anything that wonderful."

She stood on tiptoe and kissed him lightly on the cheek, then went inside, closing the door gently behind her.

As he drove home, his mind felt strangely empty, as if he were no longer capable of thought. His senses were dulled, all feeling temporarily absent.

It wasn't until he walked into his house that he began to feel again. And then what he felt was absolute, limitless loneliness rising up to engulf him.

Chapter Nine

Afternoon, ladies. How's it goin'?" the mailman asked as he deposited a small stack of mail on the counter.

Caroline found it hard to meet Jack's broad smile and twinkling blue eyes. It was the middle of September. They had been in business for a month, and they weren't doing very well.

She and Marcia had seen Jack nearly every day during that time and had begun to think of him as a friend. Suppressing an almost irresistible urge to cry on Jack's shoulder, Caroline assumed a confidence she didn't feel.

"Okay."

Jack gave her an unexpectedly shrewd look. "Just okay?"

Marcia and Caroline exchanged a look, then Marcia said unhappily, "There's no point in pretending. We haven't exactly taken the town by storm."

"Is business that bad?" Jack asked with real concern in his voice.

Both Caroline and Marcia nodded silently.

"Well, maybe you just need to do a little more advertising. If people don't know about you, they won't come in."

"We've had an ad in the Home and Garden section of the paper every week," Caroline responded.

"Well, I can't believe anyone could come in here and see these pretty dolls and not buy one."

"That's the problem," Caroline explained. "Actually, most of the people who come in, do buy something. But there just aren't that many people coming in."

Marcia added, "If advertising doesn't work, what does?"

Jack scratched his chin thoughtfully. "I don't know what to tell you. Except maybe the ads aren't reaching the right people, people with money who can afford to buy something special like your dolls."

"I suppose you see a lot of small businesses go under," Marcia commented reluctantly.

Jack's response was firm. "You ladies aren't going under."

Marcia favored him with her warmest smile. "We appreciate your confidence in us. Unfortunately, I'm afraid it may be misplaced."

"I don't think so. You're too nice." He glanced at Caroline and added, "Both of you are too nice to fail. You deserve better than that."

Caroline smiled wryly. "That's a kind thought, but I'm afraid niceness isn't necessarily related to success in business."

"By the way, we've got some coffee brewing in the back," Marcia interjected. "Would you like a cup, Jack?"

"Unfortunately, I don't have time today. Can I take a rain check?"

"Anytime."

"Thanks. By the way, I've got to buy a birthday present for my niece. I thought one of these dolls would be just the thing. Could you help me pick out one?"

Marcia and Caroline exchanged a look of perfect understanding.

Marcia said, "That's very kind, Jack, but we're not down to accepting charity."

"Who's talking about charity? I need a present for my niece. Honest."

Marcia grinned. "You're a bad liar, but a good friend, and we appreciate it. Now finish your round, and when you come in tomorrow I'll have some homemade oatmeal cookies to go with that coffee."

He met her look, smiled sheepishly, then left.

"What a nice man," Marcia commented when he'd gone.

"He sure is."

"No matter how bad a day we're having, I always feel better after talking to him."

"I know. He has such an upbeat personality, the kind of person who always finds a silver lining in every dark cloud."

"Well," Marcia responded with a sigh, "speaking of silver linings, there's one advantage to not being too busy. We can go out to lunch together. How about it? Want to close up shop for an hour and go someplace nice?"

"You mean skip the local sandwich shop? I'm not sure my stomach would recognize a decent lunch at this point."

"All the more reason to do it. Come on, let's play hooky," Marcia urged.

Caroline grinned. "Sure, why not?"

As they locked up and headed toward Marcia's car, she went on, "Want to come over tonight and help me bake those cookies I promised Jack?"

"You mean just like all those Saturday nights in high school when neither of us had a date?"

"Yeah."

"I would, but Rafe asked me to go to some function with him." Suddenly a thought occurred to her as they got into Marcia's car. "Are you baking those cookies especially for Jack?"

"Sure. Why?"

"Marcia, do you like him?"

"Of course, I like him. We both do. He's very nice."

"Don't be obtuse. You know very well what I mean."

"What do you mean?" Marcia parried, making a point of watching the road so that she didn't have to meet Caroline's piercing look.

"Like, as in the way we used it in high school. Are you interested in him?"

"Of course not, don't be ridiculous."

"What's ridiculous about it?"

"Well…" Marcia searched for an answer. Finally, she said irritably, "Well, it's ridiculous."

"Because he's a mailman?"

"Of course not! There's nothing wrong with being a mailman."

Marcia's tone held an undercurrent of anger, which proved to Caroline that she'd hit a nerve. She went on in a softer voice, "I agree there's nothing wrong with being a mailman. That's why I'm wondering why you're so reluctant to admit you're attracted to Jack."

Flashing a quick, nervous glance at Caroline, Marcia asked, "Does it show? Oh, God, I don't want to make a fool out of myself."

"Hey, you're not making a fool out of yourself. By the way, pull in over there."

"There? At that drive-in restaurant?"

"Yes."

"But—"

"Come on, do it before you go past it."

"Okay." Marcia turned her Cadillac into an empty space at the drive-in.

"Why on earth do you want to eat here? I thought we were going someplace nice."

"We were. But if we go into some nice restaurant you might feel inhibited about talking with other people around."

"What makes you think there's anything to talk about?"

At that moment the carhop interrupted their conversation to take their order. Leaning over so that she could speak to the teenage girl through the driver's window of the car, Caroline said, "Two cheeseburgers, one without onions, and two diet Cokes, please."

Then, as the girl left, she went on, "I've been noticing how you always make a point of being in the shop about the time he's due. And when you see him coming you glance in the mirror to check your hair and makeup. Plus, you're always happier after you've talked to him, kind of glowing."

Marcia groaned. "I knew it. I must look ridiculous."

"Now stop that. You don't look ridiculous and you're not making a fool of yourself. Those are subtle things that nobody else would notice."

"I hope not. God, it would be so embarrassing if Jack knew."

"Why?"

At that moment the carhop returned with their food, and Marcia waited until the girl had hooked the tray onto the car window and left before answering.

As she handed Caroline her cheeseburger—without onions—and Coke, she said, "Well, I just feel that I'm being silly. Imagine, lusting after a man I talk to for two or three minutes six days a week."

Caroline grinned. "Lusting after him, huh?"

Marcia blushed. "I know he isn't drop-dead handsome, but he has that cuddly teddy bear-look that gets more and more appealing the longer you look at him. Don't you think?"

"I do. So what do you intend to do about it?"

"What do you mean, do about it?"

"I mean, what are you going to do to consummate your lust?" Caroline said in a half teasing, half-serious tone.

Marcia giggled. "What am I supposed to do, tackle him the next time he comes in?"

"Not a bad idea. With that heavy bag over his shoulder, he'd be easy to tackle."

At Marcia's startled look, Caroline laughed and went on, "Just kidding. After all, that wouldn't be very subtle. But you can let him know you're interested."

"How?"

"Invite him over for dinner."

Marcia looked petrified. "Oh, I couldn't do that!"

"Why not?"

"What if he's not interested in me?"

"Marcia, I've seen the way he acts around you. When he comes into the shop, he makes a beeline for you, not me. The other day I held out my hand to take the mail from him and he walked right past me to hand it to you. I honestly don't think he even saw me."

"Do you really think he's interested in me?"

"I do."

"But what if he isn't? What if I invite him over for dinner and he says no?"

"Then you'll understand how men have always felt when we've rejected them."

Sighing, Marcia put her cheeseburger, which she'd hardly touched, back on the tray. "I can't do it. The man's supposed to make the first move. It's humiliating, or...or pushy for a woman to do that."

"Marcia, this isn't the nineteen sixties and you're not seventeen. Times have changed. It's okay for a woman to make the first move."

Marcia eyed her skeptically. "That's easy to say. I'll bet you couldn't do it either."

Caroline smiled shyly. "Actually, I did."

Surprise and admiration transformed Marcia's unhappy expression. "You didn't!"

"I did."

"How? When? What happened?"

Caroline laughed softly. "Slow down. It's not all that titillating a story, actually."

"Was it up in San Francisco?"

Caroline nodded. "Just before I moved down here. I didn't date at all until my divorce was final. I just plain wasn't interested. There was so much else to deal with— putting the house on the market and dealing with Realtors and potential buyers, straightening out the financial mess Edward and I were in, and trying to make it all okay for Marina, who took it hard."

Marcia nodded in understanding. "Of course. The last thing you needed at that point was something that could add to your stress."

"Exactly. Then, about a month after the divorce was final, I was sitting home on a Saturday night feeling incredibly bored. I wanted to go out. But I didn't feel like a night out with the girls. I wanted to be with a man, to dress up for him and have him take me somewhere expensive and elegant and tell me I looked wonderful and was every bit as attractive as I was before the divorce."

"So what did you do?"

"I called my periodontist."

"Your what?"

"Periodontist. That's a dentist who specializes in gum disease."

"I know what it is, I go to one every four months. What I mean is, why did you call *him*?"

Caroline grinned. "He was single. He was my age. He was very, very nice. And over the ten years or so that I'd been seeing him, we'd become good friends."

"Were you attracted to him?"

"Only mildly. But I wasn't looking for marriage or even an affair. I just wanted to go out, preferably with someone I felt comfortable with."

"So what happened?"

"I told him that I was entering the dating market for the first time in over twenty years and was nervous about it. And I wanted my first date to be with someone whose company I was sure I would enjoy."

"That must have been very flattering to him," Marcia commented.

"Of course it was. It was also true."

"So how did it work out?"

"Great. He took me to my favorite restaurant and then we went dancing, and we both had a marvelous time."

"Did you go out with him again after that?"

"Several times, until I moved back here."

Marcia was clearly dying to ask something else, but was reluctant to do so. Reading her thoughts, Caroline went on, "I didn't sleep with him. The chemistry just wasn't there. I don't know why."

"I do. The chemistry wasn't there because you never got over Rafe. *He* was the one you wanted, not your periodontist. Not even Edward, really."

It was so obviously true that Caroline didn't bother to deny it.

"What's happening with you two?" Marcia asked.

Caroline was thoughtful for a moment. Finally, she answered slowly, "I'm not really sure what's happening. We seem to have established a pattern. We go out to dinner or movies or one of the social functions he has to attend occasionally. Then we go back to my place. But he doesn't stay all night. And except for that one time, he hasn't taken me back to his house."

"It sounds kind of impersonal, in a strange way."

"It is." She didn't add that the lovemaking was anything but impersonal. It was positively torrid.

"Are you in love?"

"I don't know." At Marcia's skeptical look, she went on quickly, "I mean that. I just don't know. The man gets to me. He's in my blood. I admit that. And I know I get to him in the same way. But as for love . . ."

She let the thought trail off, incomplete.

"You don't want to love him, do you?" Marcia said with that unexpected perception that was such a contrast to her usual breezy, funny style.

Caroline shook her head. "No. I don't want to love him. And I'm absolutely sure he doesn't want to love me."

"But he pursued you so forcefully. He wouldn't let you get away."

"No he wouldn't. He wanted me, it's true, but that's not necessarily the same thing as love."

She looked pensive for a moment, then continued, "Sometimes I get the feeling there's something else going on, something I don't understand."

"What do you mean?"

"I don't know. That's just it. It's strange. It's almost like an instinctive feeling, but it's very vague."

She shook her head in frustration. Then she went on, "But getting back to you and Jack, what are you going to do?"

"Nothing."

"Marcia."

"I know, I know," she responded defensively, "it's the 1980s, times have changed and I should make the first move. But I can't. I just can't. I would feel so awful if he thought I was chasing him."

"He won't think that. He'll be flattered that a woman as attractive as you would be interested in him."

"You can't be sure of that. Caroline, I don't want to talk about it anymore. Let's talk about the shop. What are we going to do to drum up some business?"

Caroline hesitated, unsure whether she should let Marcia change the subject or not. Finally, sensing that Marcia wasn't ready to be assertive where Jack was concerned, she decided to table the subject for the moment. Jack wasn't leaving. Marcia would be seeing him for the foreseeable future and would have plenty of opportuni-

ties to approach him if she began to feel more coura-
geous.

As they drove back to the shop, they talked about the
problems they were having in attracting the right clien-
tele, but neither had any new ideas to offer. They couldn't
afford to do more advertising than they were already
doing. And even if they could, Caroline wasn't at all
convinced that would help.

Though neither said so, the unspoken understanding
was that they had six weeks left to make their venture
work. If they weren't at least breaking even by the time
their lease was up at the end of October, then The Dollhouse would be out of business.

Marcia would go back to her boring job at her cousin's dress shop, feeling that she had made her one and
only attempt at finding real fulfillment. And Caroline
would list her house for sale and take whatever menial
job she could find.

That evening Caroline and Rafe entered the large
mansion in the prestigious Van Ness Extension area
where a fund-raising party was being held for a local
congressman. Rafe was heavily involved in politics, especially with causes that related to the needs of minori-
ties in the valley, and this was only one of many such
affairs he'd taken Caroline to.

As always, she thought, Rafe looked wonderful in his
expertly cut clothes—a navy-blue blazer, matching slacks
and a blue-and-white striped shirt with a conservative tie.

In the large foyer, with its cathedral ceiling and curv-
ing staircase straight out of *Gone With the Wind*, was a
tall mirror. Caroline caught a glimpse of herself and Rafe
before they stepped into the receiving line to greet their
host. In the mirror, their appearance was striking—Rafe,

slim and dark and intense, a head taller than Caroline, who was fair and ethereal looking in a knee length, silver and white beaded silk chiffon dress.

They made an eye-catching couple—him so dark, her so fair—complete opposites of each other. As Caroline stepped forward to take their host's outstretched hand, she thought of the old cliché "opposites attract." Was that the explanation for the magnetism between them, she wondered?

Then she was pulled into the crowd of people and was too caught up in various conversations to dwell anymore on the reasons for her irresistible attraction to Rafe and his to her.

After an hour of cocktail party chitchat, Caroline was bored to tears and ready to leave. She didn't enjoy politics as Rafe did. He was tough enough to handle the backbiting, the competitiveness, the ruthlessness that existed even among people in the same party. But she found it disillusioning and had long since decided to limit her political involvement to doing her duty as a citizen and voting in elections.

Caroline was standing in a quiet corner of the vast living room sipping a club soda, when Rafe returned to her. He'd been deep in a private conversation with the congressman for half an hour and now he apologized for leaving Caroline on her own.

She smiled mischievously. "Oh, it's okay. It's been educational. I heard all the gossip about everyone who isn't here tonight. Of course, since I don't know any of the people who were being talked about, it wasn't as interesting as it could have been. I think there's more free-floating venom in this room tonight than in all the rest of Fresno and Clovis combined."

"That's the worst of these affairs. The gossip. You'd think there'd be a lot of high-minded discussions of political subjects, but there isn't."

"Of course not. It's much more fun to talk about who's sleeping with whom rather than the national debt."

He smiled dryly. "All right, you've made your point. No more politics. I don't enjoy the social part of politics myself, but it's a necessary evil. Ready to go?"

"Definitely."

They found their host, thanked him for a lovely evening and left. As Rafe drove Caroline home, he said, "Let's talk about you instead of politics. How's the business going?"

"Maybe we should go back to politics. It's infuriating but it isn't depressing."

She had tried to make her tone light and joking but didn't succeed.

Rafe gave her a long, concerned look. "That bad?"

She nodded. "But as that sportscaster said about a football game, it isn't over till it's over. We have six weeks to make something happen. And I'm determined that we're going to."

"I admire your perseverance. I mean that."

She could see that he did. His look was for once warm and unguarded as his eyes met hers. She felt oddly touched that he would compliment her in that way. She looked away, suddenly shy.

He said carefully, "Caroline, if I can help—"

"No!" Realizing how curt that sounded, she added more politely, "No, thank you. I appreciate the offer, really, but I couldn't accept."

"Why not?"

Because you already have far too much of a hold over me, she wanted to say.

Instead, she said in a firm voice, "Marcia and I will make it on our own or not at all."

"You're being stubborn and proud."

"No, I'm being realistic. If there isn't a market for my dolls, we need to learn that now before we invest further and end up losing more."

She didn't tell him that actually she had nothing left to lose. She didn't want him to know how high the stakes were for her in this venture. If she failed, he would feel sorry for her. And she felt she could handle anything from him except his pity.

"If you change your mind . . ."

"I won't."

He looked at her. "No, I don't imagine you will."

"Let's talk about your business. How's it going?"

"Fine."

"What are you working on?" she pressed, determined to change the subject.

"An office building on Shaw Avenue. It's the biggest thing we've ever done. We just broke ground yesterday."

"You must be excited."

"Jim, my partner, certainly is. He's like a little kid who's showing off for the grown-ups. It's his big opportunity to show the architectural establishment of Fresno what he can do on a grand scale, rather than being limited to the small office buildings and little corner shopping centers we've done up until now."

"I can understand his pride. I imagine you must be pretty proud yourself."

He smiled. "I must admit I am. Shaw's the most prestigious business address in town. Building something there means we've made it. We're in the big league of major developers here. Want to come by and see it once we really get started?''

It was the first time he had involved her, in any way, in his work, and she felt it was significant somehow. "I'd love to," she replied eagerly.

"In a month or so there'll be something halfway interesting to see. At the moment there's just bare ground. I'll let you know when to stop by."

"Okay."

He leaned toward her and ran one finger lightly down her cheek. "In the meantime, how would you like to go to Acapulco?"

For a moment she thought she'd heard him wrong.

"What?"

He kept his eyes on the darkened street and repeated, "I said, 'How would you like to go to Acapulco?' A simple *sí* or no will do."

"Rafe, there's nothing simple about taking off for Acapulco. At least not for me."

"Have you ever been there?"

"No."

"Then that settles it. No one should go through life without going to Acapulco at least once. We leave Friday night."

Caroline was flustered, confused and pleased, all at once. She had no idea how to react to the sudden invitation. "You're being silly, which isn't like you, and domineering, which is."

A rueful smile showed a flash of white teeth against his dark complexion. "The lady knows me entirely too well. Nevertheless, we're going to Acapulco this weekend. I'll have you back by Monday morning, so don't worry that you're being transplanted permanently. It's just a brief vacation, actually."

"But the shop..."

"Marcia can handle it."

That was all too true. Marcia would have no problem handling the meager flow of customers. Still, Caroline knew that she was being managed, and she wasn't sure she liked that one bit.

"*Rafe*..."

They had pulled up in her driveway.

Rafe turned to her, interrupting what threatened to be a flood of protest. "Aren't you going to invite me in for coffee?"

Taken aback, she asked, "Do you really want coffee?"

His voice was husky. "Of course not. But I want to come in. I thought you might prefer that polite reason rather than the real one."

She felt a delicious thrill race up her spine as he looked at her intently.

Her own voice was soft as she responded. "What's the real reason?"

His eyes glinted quicksilver in the light of a passing car, before darkness engulfed the interior of the Jaguar once again. Resting one arm on the back of the seat behind Caroline, he leaned toward her. His voice was a seductive whisper in the darkness.

"I want to strip off that dazzling dress and taste every inch of your bare skin."

"Every inch?"

"Every inch."

"And then?" There was teasing laughter in her voice, but also breathlessness as her body responded to the promise of ecstasy in his husky tone.

"And then I intend to love you thoroughly and well."

"I think . . ." She paused, then finished in a whisper, "I think I prefer the real reason." She finished in her most well mannered tone, "Won't you come inside, Mr. Marin?"

"Why, thank you, Ms. Turner, I'd love to."

He spent most of the remainder of the night doing exactly as he'd promised.

Chapter Ten

Late Friday night they arrived at Las Brisas, one of the most luxurious of Acapulco's many luxurious hotels. It overlooked the broad sweep of Acapulco Bay. Myriad lights from all the hotels ringing the bay twinkled brightly, and the black night sky was lit by a thousand stars.

"Oh, Rafe, it's marvelous!" Caroline said as their taxi drove up to the hotel.

"Las Brisas has private villas. That's why I chose it. It's very secluded."

"And very romantic," Caroline added in a whisper.

Running his fingertip lightly across her cheek, he responded huskily, "Anywhere is romantic with you. Even a mountain meadow."

Just then the doorman opened the door of their taxi and they alighted in the drive-in reception lounge. They were immediately handed tequila coolers to sip while their luggage was taken care of. A cool breeze blew in off the bay, which glistened like ebony glass on this balmy night.

A bellhop took their luggage and led them to their casita, a small but opulently furnished villa. He pointed out a refrigerator stocked with platters of fresh fruit and soft drinks and a bar filled with liquor.

"So this is how the other half lives," Caroline quipped, grinning mischievously at Rafe.

"Have you been here before *señor, señorita*?" the bellhop asked.

Caroline shook her head, and was relieved to see that Rafe did the same. Somehow, she didn't like to think that she was only the latest of many other women he'd brought to this place.

The bellhop went on in heavily accented English, "Then let me explain how we serve you. If you will let us know what time is convenient for you, we will bring hot rolls and coffee to your room. The hotel has its own seaside beach club, La Concha, which is exclusively for guests of Las Brisas. If I may be of service in any way, please do not hesitate to let me know. All of us on the staff of Las Brisas wish to help make your stay with us a pleasurable one."

It would certainly be that, Caroline thought happily.

When the bellhop left, after pocketing a suitable tip from Rafe, Caroline put her arms around Rafe and smiled up at him. "You sure know how to show a girl a good time."

He laughed. "You ain't seen nothin' yet, lady. Let's go out for a drink."

"Okay, but let me change first."

She had worn a comfortable pantsuit for the flight down from Fresno. She changed out of that into a sleeveless white silk dress with a matching jacket, changed her plain gold earrings for some pearl studs, and was ready to go.

Rafe, in the meantime, changed into a beige linen blazer over matching slacks, with a white shirt that he left open at the throat. He looked striking without being at all flashy. As they walked into the outdoor patio bar a few minutes later, Caroline felt proud to be with him. He had an air of quiet good taste that was much more appealing than some of the other men there, who wore diamond pinkie rings and gold chains.

After they had sat down at a small table and ordered margaritas, Caroline asked teasingly, "Would you ever wear a pinkie ring?"

"Never. Would you ever go out with a man who wore one?"

"Never."

Both laughed, then Caroline went on, "Rafe, this is like a fantasy come true. I feel like I've been whisked off on a magic carpet to paradise. Nothing to worry about... nothing to do but be waited on and be a complete hedonist."

"That's what Acapulco's for. To give in to all our most self-indulgent impulses. To be pampered. To forget about the real world for a while."

"Ah, yes, the real world—The Dollhouse, work, money, all those sordid things."

"Which you're not going to even think about until Monday."

Caroline smiled happily. "Right. For two days and three nights I won't think of anything but..." She hesitated, gave him a meaningful look, then finished in a husky whisper, "Pleasure."

His smile was warm and inviting. "I'll see to it that you think of nothing else."

Caroline felt a shiver of anticipation and knew that Rafe felt the same.

The waiter brought their drinks, and Rafe paid for them absently, his attention entirely on Caroline. Each took a slow sip of the golden liquid in the salt-rimmed glasses. But their eyes remained locked on each other.

Across the patio a pianist began playing softly. Caroline didn't recognize the tune, and her mind was too befuddled to concentrate on it anyway. But it was sweet and haunting and romantic.

Around them couples got up to dance. "Shall we join them?" Caroline asked, with an odd little catch in her voice.

Slowly Rafe shook his head. "I'm not in a mood to dance at this moment, Caroline."

"Ah . . . what are you in a mood to do, then?"

"Instead of telling you, I'd rather show you. In our room."

Her lips curved in a wicked smile. "But we haven't finished our drinks."

"To hell with the drinks."

She said nothing more. Instead, they both rose and walked out of the patio. Looking at their nearly untouched drinks, the waiter smiled knowingly. He served a lot of lovers at Las Brisas.

Just after dawn the next morning, Caroline rose, slipped on a satin robe, and walked out onto the villa's patio. Brightly colored exotic flowers floated in their private pool. She smiled wryly at the thought of such opulence.

Walking over to the waist-high adobe wall on the edge of the terraced hillside, Caroline looked out. In the distance was the breathtaking sweep of Acapulco Bay.

Mountains and promontories surrounded the tall luxury hotels that crowded the bay, while perfect white beaches formed a crescent around the vivid blue water.

It was even more dazzling than Caroline had expected—the clear sunlight, richly colorful flowers and the water itself, bluer than any Caroline had ever seen. Suddenly she was seized by a feeling of excitement. Turning, she went back into the room, and found Rafe sprawled in the center of the king-size bed, a white sheet loosely covering him from the waist down. He was still asleep, but he was just beginning to stir.

Lying down beside him, Caroline blew softly on his ear.

"Time to wake up, sleepyhead."

He groaned tiredly and without opening his eyes asked, "What time is it?"

"Six o'clock."

His eyes flew open. "Six! Caroline, that's practically the middle of the night." Reaching out, he pulled her against him, closed his eyes again, and finished, "Let's go back to sleep."

"Let's not. Oh, Rafe, there's so much to see and do. I want to go down to the beach, and fly on one of those hang gliders pulled by a boat, and see the high divers—"

"Hold on," Rafe interrupted her, laughing. "You don't have to do it all before breakfast."

"But I want to get started. I feel like a little kid on Christmas Eve; I can't wait for all the excitement to begin."

"Okay. I can see sleep is out of the question. All right, lady. Your personal guided tour of Acapulco will begin right after I bury my face in those hot rolls and coffee the bellhop promised. I'm *starving* this morning. Somehow I worked up quite an appetite last night."

Ignoring his sly grin, Caroline got up from the bed.

"I'll call room service now." She walked toward the phone. Pausing by the refrigerator, she opened it and pulled out a deep red apple. "In the meantime, how's this for a munchie?"

She tossed it to Rafe, who caught it easily. "It'll do," he murmured, biting into it as he ambled slowly into the bathroom.

After breakfast they went for an early morning swim in the ocean that was far warmer and clearer than the water Caroline was familiar with off the California coast.

Then they took one of the jeeps provided by the hotel and drove down to the town. Rafe took Caroline to the cathedral first. With its big blue spires, it looked more like a Russian Orthodox church than a Catholic one. Then they wandered through the shops and boutiques of the *zocalo*, the old town square. Rafe spoke fluent Spanish and Caroline let him do all the bargaining for the things she wanted to buy.

Late that afternoon they returned to the hotel, laden with purchases. They changed back into their bathing suits and went down to the beach. Caroline's courage failed her and she wanted to back out of the ride through the air in a hang glider pulled by a motorboat. But Rafe persuaded her to try the thrilling ride. She was terrified as the parachute pulled her higher and higher into the air until she was above the roofs of the hotels. Then, forcing herself to relax, she gradually began to actually enjoy the ride, especially the view as all of Acapulco lay spread out below her.

That evening they sat on the patio of a restaurant where they had just eaten spicy shrimp *diablo* and fresh corn tortillas made by a little old woman who sat in an alcove patting the cornmeal into flat round tortillas, then frying them quickly on a hot grill. Nearby, the famous high-divers jumped from a tiny ledge on a steep cliff into the thrashing surf of La Quebrada, hundreds of feet below. The gorge was lit by floodlights, and after each dive the divers climbed back up the cliff, dripping and smiling, gathering money from the thrilled onlookers.

Caroline took a sip of the surprisingly potent coconut milkshake, *coco preparado*, and asked, "How can they do it? I'd be absolutely terrified."

"They do it for the same reason most people do things—for money. They're well-paid. In a poverty-stricken country like Mexico, it isn't hard to find people willing to risk their lives to earn a decent living."

There was an edge to Rafe's voice that hadn't been there before. Caroline realized with a start that she had completely forgotten a crucial fact—part of Rafe's roots were in this country. His family on his father's side had come from here. He might very well joke about Acapulco being a playground for the wealthy, but Mexico as a whole meant more to him than that.

"Rafe, what part of Mexico did your father's people come from?" she asked tentatively.

She was afraid he would refuse to answer because the subject was such a personal one. To her relief, he answered slowly, "From Ensenada, on the Baja California coast. My father was born in the San Joaquin Valley, but his mother came from Mexico after the turn of the century."

"With her family?"

"No. Alone."

Caroline was intrigued. "But she must have been young. Why would she have come alone to a new country?"

"She came looking for her husband. He'd come up to the valley to work because there was no way he could support his wife in Ensenada. When she stopped hearing from him and several weeks went by, she decided something must be very wrong. So she put her meager possessions in one battered suitcase and began walking to California."

Imagining what Rafe's grandmother must have felt—alone, probably speaking no English, unsure if her husband was alive or dead—touched Caroline profoundly.

"She must have been very brave."

"She was. She nearly starved, but she didn't give up. When she finally got to Clovis, she found my grandfather sick and nearly dead. She nursed him back to health and worked as a farm laborer until he was well enough to work again."

For the first time, Caroline truly understood the determination that drove Rafe. It was in his blood, a vital force in a family that wouldn't give up, that was bent on surviving at all costs.

"You must be very proud of your family," she said softly.

His gray eyes opened wide in surprise. Clearly he hadn't expected that comment from her. When he answered her, it was with a touch of defiance. "I am. Very proud."

For several minutes neither said anything else. Caroline was no longer interested in the high-divers. In his own way, the compelling man sitting next to her had even more courage than those reckless daredevils.

Why then, she wondered poignantly, hadn't he been brave enough to face parenthood as a teenager? But that was a question that could never be answered.

As they returned to the hotel that night, Caroline was subdued. Acapulco's glitter had worn just a bit thin.

But the next morning her spirits revived as they went on a cruise up one of the rivers that flowed from the interior out to the ocean. It wasn't exactly a rugged excursion. Arranged by the hotel for several of the guests, it featured a mobile bar and *mariachi* musicians whose music seemed strangely out of place in the jungle.

The boat slid gently into the jungle, penetrating the wilder, undeveloped area of Acapulco. Caroline couldn't decide which was more dramatically colorful, the tropical birds or the sunset. The birds squawked from the thick trees. Obviously they were angry at the invasion of their normally quiet, uninhabited territory.

It was after dark when Caroline and Rafe returned to their room. Both were tired and somehow reluctant to go out again. Instead, Rafe ordered dinner from room service, and they spent their final evening in Acapulco dining alone in front of a flickering fire in the adobe fireplace. A cold breeze was blowing in off the ocean that night, and the fire was warm and welcome.

Picking up his glass of wine, Rafe made a toast. "To the nicest weekend I've had in a long time."

Smiling, Caroline raised her glass to his. Though she didn't say so, she didn't exactly agree with his choice of adjectives. For her, the weekend had been many things—exciting, passionate, relaxing, interesting. Even a little poignant at times. She knew that she would never forget the past two days and three nights, no matter what happened to her budding relationship with Rafe.

Very early the next morning Caroline lay in a lounge chair by the private pool, taking one last look at the fabulous view. She would miss Acapulco. As she had said when they'd first arrived, it was, indeed, like a fantasy come true.

Amidst all the frankly decadent luxury and natural beauty, there was only one disquieting element. Though most of the time Rafe was happy and relaxed in a way he hadn't been in Clovis, at times he seemed preoccupied and moody. He seemed to be wrestling with an inner problem that he refused to confide to Caroline.

His moodiness seemed to descend when they were particularly close and loving. At those times, when they'd just made love or talked intimately in a way that Rafe had been loathe to do before, Caroline could almost see the barriers go up. His expression became distant, his tone guarded. And then she knew he had retreated from her once again.

But despite that, it had truly been a magical weekend. Caroline hadn't realized just how much stress she'd been under with starting the shop, then worrying about its failure. Over these three days she had relaxed completely, in a way she hadn't done since her marriage ended. Though she wished they didn't have to leave Acapulco in only a scant two hours, she knew she would return to work recharged, revitalized, ready to tackle the problems the business faced.

Suddenly strong arms encircled her waist. A deeply masculine voice, still thick with sleep, said, "Good morning, *señorita*."

Caroline looked up at Rafe as he sat down next to her on the lounge. He hadn't bothered to put on a robe. After all, in their secluded villa, no one could see them. Only modesty had prompted her to slip on her short white terry cloth robe before coming outside.

Now, looking at his naked body, Caroline felt the same secret, breathless thrill that she always felt when she saw him like this. His chest was broad and hard, smooth except for a patch of darkly matted hair high in the center. The muscles in his shoulders and arms were strongly corded from daily workouts with weights.

Everything about him was very male, very earthy, very sensuous. He exuded raw sexual power; like a lean, dark panther, quiet yet lethal in his effect on her.

"Have you enjoyed the weekend?" he asked.

She smiled. "You know I have. It's fun to be decadent for a while, to be waited on and catered to. In short, to see how the other half lives."

"They live very well, especially here."

Sighing she said, "But by noon I'll be back in the real world. And when I wait on customers or do housework, this will just be a wonderful memory."

"We don't have time to go into the restaurant. Shall I order breakfast from room service?"

Caroline nodded, but something in her expression caught his attention and he made no move to go.

"On the other hand," he said slowly, "maybe a swim would be a better idea. How about it? One last time?"

"Okay. I'll put on my swimsuit," she said as she started to rise.

"Don't bother." He picked her up and said with a laugh, "I'll help you in."

"Rafael Marin, don't you dare throw me in!" Caroline shouted just before he unceremoniously dumped her in the warm, clear water.

As she rose to the top of the water, her robe floating soggily around her, she saw him dive in after her.

He came up only a few feet from her, then swam over to her.

"You don't need this," he said, taking the soaking wet robe off her and tossing it onto the edge of the pool.

She stood naked before him. Judging by the smoldering look in his eyes, she knew she was affecting him at that moment as he was affecting her. He pulled her against him and the slippery feel of their bodies in the warm water was incredibly erotic.

"I thought we were going to swim," she teased breathlessly.

"I have a better idea."

He drew her to the steps, then carried her out of the pool and into the bedroom where the bed was still disheveled from their lovemaking of the night before. Putting her down on the bed, he covered her wet body with his own. Caroline felt a delicious thrill of anticipation as her soft breasts were crushed beneath him.

As her hips pushed against his, she felt a hard, throbbing pressure between her legs. She slipped her leg between his and her mouth rose to meet his as he kissed her deeply.

She heard a low groan deep in his throat, then his hands were all over her, exploring the secret places they'd come to know so intimately. Her back arched at his touch, her breathing grew ragged. At the same time they continued kissing eagerly as if they couldn't taste enough of each other.

He moved and for one tantalizing second his body was poised over hers. Then they were joined, and the gentle rocking motion quickly grew more frenzied.

And then came the fire...like molten lava pouring through her body, until she could bear no more, she was carried on the crest of that fiery wave for one endless moment before slowly coming down to earth again.

For a while they lay there together, neither speaking. Caroline knew she should get up, pack, and get ready to go to the airport for the return flight to Fresno. But she didn't want to move. All she could think of was that this was the last time they would make love in this magical place.

She was haunted by an irrational feeling that they would never return here, never make love here again. She told herself she was being ridiculous, but she couldn't shake the feeling.

"Rafe?"

"Mmm?" he mumbled, nuzzling her cheek affectionately.

"This has been the happiest three days I've ever known."

There was a silence and she felt him pull back, both emotionally and physically. She didn't understand it, but she knew that was what had just happened.

"Thank you," she whispered awkwardly.

"Don't thank me." His voice was tight and she sensed that he had to force himself not to sound angry.

Turning so that she could face him, she asked the question that had been bothering her on and off all weekend. "What's wrong?"

"It's getting late. We'll have to hurry to make the plane."

As he started to rise, she gripped his shoulder, stopping him. "That isn't what's wrong."

For a moment his eyes locked with hers. In their gray depths she saw a struggle going on, a struggle that she didn't begin to understand.

Then he said slowly, as if the words were torn from his very soul, "I . . . don't . . . want . . . to . . . love . . . you."

Letting go of his arm, she lay back on the pillow and breathed a soft sigh of relief. So that was it. She had been so afraid it was something else, something much worse. Though she hadn't been consciously aware of it, she realized then that all weekend she had half expected him to say that it was over between them, and the trip was just an elegant way of ending the affair.

Now she smiled up at him as he sat on the edge of the bed. "I don't want to love you, either. I'm terrified by what I feel for you. So why don't we just let things go on as they were as long as . . . as long as this is what we both want."

For a moment Caroline saw two opposing emotions warring on his countenance—relief and disappointment.

Then he said carefully, "All right. We'll let things go on as they are. For now . . ."

Then he rose from the bed and went into the bathroom. A second later, she heard the shower come on, and she knew that Rafe wouldn't repeat this conversation again. She should feel relieved, she knew, considering what she'd just said to him. God knew it was true. She didn't want to love him, didn't want him to love her.

Or did she? a tiny, nagging voice deep within asked mischievously.

It was certainly true that she felt a sharp disappointment completely at odds with her brave words.

But it didn't matter what she felt, she realized. The subject they had just broached so awkwardly—the subject of their emotional feelings for one another, as opposed to their physical attraction—had been closed almost as soon as it had been opened.

Chapter Eleven

So how was your trip?'' Marcia asked as Caroline walked into the shop just after lunch.

"I gained three pounds and definitely decided it's better to be rich than poor."

Marcia laughed. "Sounds like you had a great time."

"I did. How did things go here?"

Marcia grimaced. "As usual, unfortunately."

At that point a customer came in, interrupting their conversation. Caroline knew that something had to be done, and fast. They were drifting inexorably toward failure, and she wasn't about to sit back and watch that happen. The hopes and dreams of both her and Marcia were tied up in The Dollhouse. Somehow there had to be a way to save it.

Marcia left early that afternoon to take care of some business at the bank. Caroline sensed that Marcia would have preferred to leave after Jack came, but she had no choice. The bank closed at three o'clock.

When Jack came in a few minutes later with the mail he looked around in surprise. "Isn't Marcia here?"

"No, she had some business to take care of. But there's coffee in the back. Want a cup?"

He shook his head. "I'd better not. I'm running behind schedule today."

Caroline knew that if Marcia had been the one making the offer, Jack would have accepted happily, no matter how far behind schedule he was. She couldn't help being rather amused at Jack's transparent attraction to Marcia.

Yet it seemed rather sad that these two people who might be right for each other wouldn't ever find out because both were too shy to make the first move.

Caroline wasn't impulsive by nature, but she decided to do something very impulsive. As Jack deposited the mail on the counter, then turned toward the door with a cheery goodbye, she stopped him.

"Jack, wait!"

When he looked back at her, she felt a sudden qualm. What if she was doing something totally stupid? Well, she wouldn't know the answer to that until she went ahead and did it.

Taking a deep breath, she said in a rush, "I think you're attracted to Marcia, and I know she's attracted to you, so why don't you ask her out?"

There was a stunned silence. Jack's expression was utterly flabbergasted as he stood facing her. Caroline's courage deserted her and she felt like a fool. Why hadn't she kept her big mouth shut? she wondered unhappily as intense embarrassment washed over her.

Then Jack spoke slowly. "I haven't asked her out because I didn't think she could be interested in someone like me."

Caroline had to work very hard to suppress a grin of delight. In as even a voice as she could muster, she responded, "What do you mean, someone like you?"

"Well, mailmen aren't known for being rich, you know. And she owns a business and drives a Cadillac. I just assumed she could do better than me."

"Do you care about her?"

He stared down at his shoes, unable to meet Caroline's look. But his voice was firm as he answered, "You bet I do."

"Would you treat her well?"

He looked up abruptly. "Of course, I would!"

"Then she couldn't do any better than that."

"Look, I know she's got to be doing a lot better than I am financially."

"Jack, she's doing all right, but she isn't rich."

"Well, anyway, it wouldn't look right."

"Oh, I see. You're more concerned with how things look than how they are."

She was purposefully trying to get a rise out of him, and it worked. His blue eyes flashed angrily for the first time since she'd known him.

"Of course not. But why would she be interested in me?"

"I don't know. You'll have to ask her that. Judging from my own experience, there are rarely logical, good reasons why one person likes another. Who can explain chemistry?"

"Caroline, I appreciate your good intentions, but I just can't believe that Marcia's interested in me. If I asked her out, it might be embarrassing for both of us."

"Well, if you don't have the guts to deal with that possibility, maybe you're right. Maybe you're not the man for her."

She hadn't intended to be quite so blunt, but she was frustrated with the unwillingness of both Jack and Marcia to take a chance. As soon as the words were out, she regretted them. But it was too late. Without saying another word, Jack turned and strode out the door.

That does it, Caroline thought miserably. She'd succeeded brilliantly at making the situation infinitely worse.

When Marcia returned a short time later, Caroline didn't have the courage to tell her what she'd done. She told herself that it would just make Marcia feel awkward around Jack if she knew that Caroline had talked to him. But the truth was, she knew Marcia would be hurt and angry, and she just couldn't face that right now.

Using a headache as an excuse, she left work early and went home.

Since she wasn't seeing Rafe that night she'd planned a quiet evening when she could catch up on mundane tasks like ironing and housework. And she had an idea she wanted to develop for a new doll, one that would be her own creation rather than a copy of an antique doll.

But now, as she changed into jeans and a light sweater, she felt no enthusiasm for any of these things. She was hit with an attack of utter depression. Nothing was going right in her life. The business was failing. Her relationship with Rafe had her on an emotional roller coaster. She'd just revealed Marcia's private feelings to Jack, which Marcia had made it clear she didn't want to do.

As she forced herself to eat a bowl of clam chowder that she didn't really want, she sank deeper and deeper into misery. A tear trickled down her cheek, then another. She was about to give way entirely to a good hard cry, when the telephone rang.

Brushing the tears from her face with a napkin, she answered it with a definite quaver in her voice.

"Hello."

"Mom, is that you?"

Quickly, she pulled herself together. "Of course, it's me. How's it going, Marina?"

"How's it going with *you*? You sound awful."

"I've just been indulging in a little self-pity. But everything's fine."

"Everything can't be fine if you're feeling sorry for yourself. That isn't like you, at all. You're the original stiff upper lip."

"I'm just being stupid. Really, everything's okay. Tell me what's happening with you."

"*Mother.*"

The tone of that "mother" was so familiar that Caroline found herself smiling.

"Come on, Mom. Let it out. You know, the advantage of having a grown-up kid instead of a child is that you don't always have to be strong."

"Is that right?" Caroline teased.

Marina laughed softly. "Yes, it is. So tell me what's wrong. Is it the business?"

"Well, we're not thriving, I admit. To be perfectly honest, if things don't turn around soon, it'll be all over for The Dollhouse. And I'll probably end up working in an office after all."

"I bet you'll pull it off, yet. You're one gutsy lady."

"Is that what I am?"

"You bet. Where do you think I got my stubborn determination from?"

"I've often wondered. Are you still living sans plumbing and electricity?"

Marina laughed. "Yes. But guess what?"

"What?"

"I finished my novel. I just typed 'The End' not five minutes ago."

"Oh, honey, that's great. I knew you'd do it."

"I haven't done anything yet. It still has to sell, or I'm just one more unpublished writer."

"It'll sell."

"You're sure of that?"

"Of course. So what are you doing to celebrate?"

"Jeff's taking me out to dinner at Nepenthe. Nothing like a busman's celebration. I got through serving lunch there three hours ago, and in a few minutes I'm going back. Only this time as a customer, not a waitress."

"Seems to me that every time we talk, you're about to go out with Jeff. Are things getting serious?"

"No way. I'm never getting married."

"I'll remind you of that as you're walking down the aisle someday."

"I mean it."

Caroline didn't tease Marina further. The fact was, she was afraid Marina did mean it. She'd taken the divorce hard—even harder, in a way, than Caroline had done. Her illusions of her parents' perfect marriage were shattered, and she'd been more than a little cynical ever since.

"Besides," Marina went on blithely, "Jeff's so establishment. He's really into being an attorney and wearing the right clothes and driving the right car. He'd actually expect me to join the Junior League."

"A fate worse than death."

"Mother." Suddenly Marina chuckled, then went on, "Okay, maybe it wouldn't be so awful for someone else, but it just isn't me."

Caroline sighed. "I know. I long ago accepted that I'd given birth to a rebel. But, remember, I was in the Junior League and we did a lot of good work."

"I know. Well, I've got to run. Jeff will be here soon and he hates to be kept waiting. If he says 'Time is money' one more time, I may do something drastic like mismatch all his socks."

"Well, have fun. And be easy on poor Jeff. Not everyone is cut out to follow the different drummer you're following."

"You know, for a mother, you're not at all objectionable."

"Thanks."

"Are you okay now?"

"Yes. Now go out and have a good time."

"I will. One thing about dating a typical conservative male chauvinist, he likes to pay for everything. It really helps my budget. Bye, Mom. I love you."

"I love you, too, sweetheart. Bye."

As she hung up, Caroline felt one hundred percent better. She had always had a close relationship with her daughter. Probably, she realized, because in the beginning it was just the two of them alone against the world. That had forged a bond that had never broken, even during Marina's turbulent teenage years.

In a better frame of mind, she decided to tackle her mail. Since she was sure it was mostly bills she hadn't bothered with it yet. Walking out to her mailbox, she brought in the small pile of envelopes and advertising circulars.

Sitting in the lounge chair out on the patio, she sorted through the mail. One piece in particular caught her eye. It was a flyer promoting a fund-raising charity auction to be held by the Junior League. It announced that local artists and craftsmen, plus local businesses, had donated some very special items.

Normally, Caroline would have tossed it aside without looking at it. But because of Marina's wry comment about the Junior League, she paused to glance at it. And as she did, an idea took shape in her mind.

She remembered Jack's comment some time earlier—"Maybe you're not reaching the right people. People with money."

Jumping up, she ran to the phone and dialed Marcia's number. She was about to hang up after the fourth ring, when Marcia finally answered.

"Marcia, it's Caroline."

"Oh, hold on a minute, I've still got cookie dough on my hands." She left, and in the background Caroline heard the sound of running water. A moment later, Marcia returned to the phone. "Sorry. You caught me right in the middle of baking."

Caroline couldn't resist asking, "Are those cookies, by any chance, for Jack?"

"Yes, but no editorial comments, please."

"Okay. I called about something else anyway. I have an idea."

"About the business?"

"Of course. What else is on our minds nowadays? Listen to this—the Junior League is having an auction to raise money for charity."

"Yes, I know. I have some friends who belong to it."

"You do? Perfect!"

"What's perfect about it?"

"Marcia, listen, local artists and craftsmen, as well as businesses have donated items."

"Are you suggesting—"

"Yes," Caroline interrupted excitedly. "Let's donate a doll. No, not a doll, *the* doll. The best we've got."

"But we'll be giving away several hundred dollars."

"We'll be getting a lot of free advertising in return. The people going to this auction are the very ones we've been trying to reach."

"You're right about that." Marcia's tone became more excited. "Oh, Carrie, I think you're on to something!"

"Will you speak to your friends about accepting our donation?"

"Sure, but don't worry. There won't be any problem. They'll be delighted to get such a special item."

"All we ask is that they let us put a prominent sign under the doll as it's displayed saying where it came from and where interested people can get more like it."

"Of course. Now what doll did you have in mind?"

"Not one of our regular stock. A new one that I'll make. The auction isn't until October fifteenth so I should just barely have enough time if I work full-time on it and leave the shop to you."

"Okay. That certainly won't be a problem with things as slow as they are. Carrie, do you think it'll help?"

"I hope so. It's our last chance. Otherwise, at the end of October we close our doors. Well, I've got to get busy making the preliminary sketch of the doll."

"What are you going to call it?"

"Marina."

Marcia laughed. "Great idea. See you tomorrow."

"Right. Bye."

When she hung up, Caroline went right to work and spent the rest of the evening drawing. By the time she went to bed, she was tired but exhilarated. Her depression was entirely gone. They might go out of business yet. But at least they would go down fighting.

The next afternoon, Friday, she made a point of getting Marcia out of the shop about the time Jack was due. Marcia was reluctant to leave, but Caroline insisted there were some special materials she needed from a nearby hobby shop, and that she really couldn't take time off from the new doll she was making to go get them.

When Jack came in a few minutes later, Caroline faced him squarely. She intended to tell him she was sorry for her rudeness of the day before and she would never poke her long nose into his or Marcia's personal life again. But before she could speak, the door opened and Marcia hurried in.

"Hi, Jack." Turning to Caroline, she handed her a bag with the things Caroline had requested. "Here you go. I was lucky, the place was practically deserted and it didn't take any time at all to get this stuff."

"Thanks," Caroline murmured unhappily. She had no idea how she could apologize to Jack without doing so in front of Marcia, which would be terribly embarrassing for all three of them.

"Well, Jack, would you like some coffee and a peanut butter cookie? I just made 'em last night."

"No." His tone was so abrupt that both Marcia and Caroline exchanged a startled look.

Before Marcia could say another word, he went on, "Recently someone made me realize what a darn fool I've been." He shot a quick meaningful look at Caroline, then finished, "It was about time, too. Marcia, will you go out to dinner with me tomorrow night?"

Marcia's mouth fell open slightly, and she simply stood there as the seconds dragged by. Finally, she responded with painful honesty, "Jack, I was sixteen the last time I went out with someone other than my late husband. I'm not sure I know how to behave on a date."

He smiled sheepishly. "It's been about that long since I went out with someone other than my late wife. I'm not sure I know what to do either. Maybe we could kind of learn together."

A slow smile spread across Marcia's round face, lighting her dark-blue eyes in a way that Caroline hadn't seen in a long, long time.

"I think that's a lovely idea. What time shall I be ready?"

"Is eight o'clock okay?"

"It's fine. But seven's even better."

He grinned. "I'll see you then."

When he left, he made a point of smiling at Caroline, who returned the smile happily.

When they were alone, Marcia turned to Caroline. "Did you say anything to Jack?"

"Yes," she admitted reluctantly, then steeled herself for her friend's anger.

"Well, I only have one thing to say to you, Caroline Turner. You're gonna have to handle the shop alone tomorrow because I'll be spending the day at the beauty shop!"

They laughed and hugged each other. Then as Caroline worked on the new doll, they talked about what Marcia should wear.

On Saturday evening, October fifteenth, Caroline felt so nervous she could hardly close the tiny pearl buttons on her white silk dress. She and Marcia were attending the Junior League charity auction to see how the response was to their doll and to talk personally to anyone who might be interested in it.

When the doorbell rang, she breathed a sigh of relief. That would be Rafe. Maybe he would have better luck with the buttons than she was having.

Opening the door, she gave him a quick hello, then turning her back to him, said, "Can you finish these damn things?"

He smiled. "I take it you're nervous."

Quickly his fingers closed the row of buttons.

"Of course I'm nervous. What if no one even bids on the doll?"

When he finished, he put his hands on her shoulders and turned her to face him. "Of course someone will bid on it. There's nothing to be nervous about. Where's the doll?"

She pointed toward an open box propped up on a nearby table. In it was the most fabulous doll Caroline had ever made. "Marina" was a fantasy brought to life. Twenty-six inches tall, she wore a royal-blue velvet gown shirred at the edges and trimmed in Norwegian snow fox and heavy chantilly lace. She wore pearl earrings and a pearl broach. Atop her carefully arranged mass of dark hair was a wide brimmed hat that swept low over one clear gray eye. Trimmed with flowers and lace, it was straight out of the Gay Nineties.

The expression on her round porcelain face was impudent and saucy—and it was straight out of a photo of her namesake, the real Marina.

Rafe gave a long, low whistle of appreciation. "This is what you've been working on night and day for the past three weeks?"

Caroline nodded.

"I can see why it took so much time and effort. But, Caroline, are you sure you want to give it away?"

"Positive. If this doesn't impress people, nothing I can do will."

"But there must be a small fortune in that doll just in her clothes."

Caroline grinned, pleased with herself. "Actually, I took pieces of some of my old clothes. The fur came off an old dinner suit that I haven't worn in years. I didn't mind losing that. But the lace . . . it's really exquisite and I must admit it hurt a little to cut it up for her dress."

Rafe gave her a thoughtful look. "You really threw yourself into this, didn't you?"

"I had to. We're down to the wire now. There couldn't be any holding back."

"No, when it comes right down to it, I can't see you holding back."

Caroline sensed there was a double entendre there, but she wasn't capable of figuring it out then.

"We'd better be going. I'm supposed to get there early so they can put the doll on display."

"What's her name?" he asked as she put the lid on the box and tucked it securely under her arm.

She hesitated. When she answered she didn't quite look at him. "Marina."

"Mmm. An elegant name for an elegant creature."

For an instant, Caroline felt a pang of sadness and anger such as she hadn't felt with Rafe in quite a while. She had never once mentioned Marina to Rafe. He didn't know that his child was a girl named Marina who was this doll's namesake.

She'd argued back and forth with herself about discussing Marina with him. But since he never asked about their child, she decided he must not want to know.

"Is Marcia coming?" he went on, unaware of Caroline's thoughts.

Caroline was glad for the change of subject. She had enough to worry about that night without falling back into all the old anguish from the past she'd resolved to put behind her.

"Oh, yes, she's coming. In fact, she's bringing her boyfriend."

"I didn't know she was involved with anyone."

"It's very recent. Actually, I'm not sure boyfriend is the right term to use. It sounds so juvenile somehow. But it's exactly what he is. They've been seeing each other a lot lately."

"I'm glad. Her husband's death was hard on her, I know. It's great that she finally found someone."

Caroline was rather surprised at Rafe's concern for Marcia. Though she had gradually discovered that he cared more about people than he liked to let on, he rarely let that caring show. It really touched her to think he cared about Marcia.

In an instant, the anger she'd begun to feel toward him again dissipated.

"You know something, Rafael Marin?"

"What, Caroline Turner?"

"Sometimes you're a nice guy."

"Well, don't tell anyone. It'll ruin my reputation. Now, let's go."

Twenty minutes later they were walking into the Hilton Hotel in downtown Fresno where the fundraiser was being held. Even though they'd arrived early, the ballroom was already crowded. It was a popular event, Caroline was glad to see. If there were a lot of people there, it was much more likely that her doll would bring a high price and get a great deal of attention.

As Caroline paused to look around, Marcia and Jack came up.

"Oh, good, you're here," Marcia exclaimed. "I was just talking to the woman who's in charge of the donated items. They're all in place and we've got to get the doll over there. She showed me where to put it. By the way, Rafael Marin this is Jack Dinwiddie."

Before the two men could exchange how-do-you-do's, Marcia went on, "Let's go. We don't want to lose one minute when our doll could be on display."

"What's going to happen?" Caroline asked as Marcia led the four of them to the area where the items to be auctioned were on display.

"The auction itself starts at nine o'clock. That gives people a good two hours to look over everything and decide what they want to bid on."

"I don't think I can stand waiting for two whole hours to find out if anyone's going to bid on it," Caroline said anxiously.

Marcia, who had seen the finished doll earlier, responded confidently, "Don't be ridiculous. The question isn't whether or not anyone's going to bid on it, but how much people will bid. It's the most gorgeous thing I've ever seen. And definitely the best thing you've done, Carrie."

"I'd like to do more of my own designs, actually. I hope I get the chance."

They put the box in the display area marked with a large card that read, The Dollhouse. Then they took off the lid, set it aside, and stepped away so they weren't obscuring the doll from the view of the people milling around. But they didn't go too far away. Both Marcia and Caroline were dying to hear any comments that might be made, and wanted to be available to answer any questions from people who might be interested in other dolls in the shop.

Caroline's nervousness was mollified as she heard the glowing comments of people admiring the doll. It attracted quite a crowd of women who talked of buying it as a special gift for a daughter or granddaughter.

Caroline's innate shyness returned full force, and she hung back, quietly sipping the glass of wine Rafe brought her from the refreshment booth. Marcia was in the thick of things, talking to anyone who seemed at all interested in the doll, explaining about the shop and the other dolls they had there.

When one woman asked if a doll could be made in the likeness of her granddaughter, Marcia answered with assurance, "Of course! My partner, who creates these exceptional dolls, can do anything."

Caroline, Rafe and Jack all exchanged amused looks at Marcia's breezy confidence.

When the auction began at precisely nine o'clock, Caroline felt the knot deep in her stomach tighten. By the time their doll was put up for bids at ten o'clock, she was desperate for the whole experience to be over.

"We will start the bidding on this lovely, handmade porcelain doll at five hundred dollars," the auctioneer began.

The doll was actually worth four times that, but Caroline wasn't concerned about its true value. She just wanted it to go for a decent price to indicate a general interest in it.

"Do I hear five hundred?" the auctioneer said in his high, singsong voice.

A hand in the audience of people around the auctioneer's podium shot up.

"Five hundred, I've got five hundred, do I hear six?" he went on.

Another hand went up.

And so it went until the auctioneer finally brought down his gavel at fifteen hundred dollars.

Caroline felt dizzy with relief. She and Marcia hugged each other, as well as hugging Jack and Rafe. "Marina" was a big success. And while there was no guarantee that success would translate into increased business for The Dollhouse, Caroline couldn't help feeling it would.

They would know for sure when they opened up on Monday.

Chapter Twelve

Business was only slightly up on Monday. The big difference was that the women who came in weren't just idle browsers, but had attended the charity auction. All of them seemed to like what they saw, and two made special orders for custom-made dolls.

As they locked up the shop that night, both Marcia and Caroline felt a tenuous optimism. *We're going to make it,* Caroline told herself again and again. Anything else was unthinkable.

Each day business improved slightly, as the women who had come in told other women about "that darling little shop with the most precious dolls."

When Jack delivered the mail on Friday, he found both Caroline and Marcia in much improved spirits.

"You must be raking in the loot," he quipped.

Marcia grinned broadly. "Not yet, but we will be if this gradual improvement keeps up."

"I just wish it was a little less gradual," Caroline added with some concern. "We've got to sign another lease by the end of next week, and right now we really don't have the money to do it."

"You'll have it by then," Jack responded confidently. "I have all the confidence in the world in both of you."

Caroline grinned ruefully. "You are a cockeyed optimist if ever there was one."

"I think Jack's right," Marcia added. "Wait till our ad appears this Sunday. I'm sure it's going to help turn things around fast."

The ad was a special one announcing that they were taking orders for Christmas. By that time in October, most other businesses had already started their Christmas advertising, and they had decided to do the same.

Turning to Marcia, Jack asked, "How about if I pick you up at seven? The movie starts at seven-thirty."

"Great. See you then."

When he left, Caroline eyed Marcia curiously. She had intended not to pry into her friend's romance, but she couldn't resist doing so now.

"So how's it going with you two?"

Marcia, who was normally outgoing and unflappable, looked uncharacteristically shy. "Oh, fine."

"Just fine?"

"Well..." Marcia actually blushed, to Caroline's surprise.

Finally, she went on, "We've been seeing a lot of each other."

"I know." Suddenly Caroline took a shot in the dark. "So when's the wedding?"

Marcia turned startled eyes to her. "Carrie, how'd you know? Did Jack say anything?"

"You mean it's true? Oh, Marcia, I'm so happy for you!"

As Caroline hugged her, Marcia protested, "Now, hold on, nothing's settled. We haven't known each other that long."

"I understand. But you obviously enjoy each other's company a lot."

"Oh, yes. Sometimes I think we're seeing too much of each other and I make a point of spending an evening alone. And oh, Carrie, I miss him so much then. I can't wait to see him again. I didn't really appreciate how lonely my life had become since Carl's death, until I met Jack. I was becoming a hermit, letting life pass me by."

"You've blossomed since you've become involved with him. You should see yourself. You actually glow."

"In a way I feel like I did when I was sixteen and had a crush on someone. Only this is even better."

Caroline knew exactly what Marcia meant. She had loved Rafe when she was a teenager, and it had been wonderful. But now that they were more mature, it was even better. It was more exciting, and much more satisfying, than when they were young and naive.

As if reading her thoughts, Marcia asked, "What about you and Rafe? Any wedding plans there?"

Caroline shook her head slowly. "Definitely not. Rafe isn't interested in commitment and neither am I. At least not with him."

"Too much history?"

"Exactly. With you and Jack it's different. You're both starting over and you can make a whole new life together. Rafe and I will always be haunted by the past."

"But I thought you decided to put the past behind you?"

Caroline's smile was humorless. "I did. But that's easier said than done. There are constant reminders. I feel myself holding back, not giving of myself as totally as I would otherwise. It's a constant push-pull. I'm drawn to him, but then something will happen to remind me of the past, and my defenses go up. I sense the same thing is happening with him."

"But what does he have to feel defensive about? You were the one who was hurt."

Caroline sighed. "Who knows? Maybe he sees what happened differently than I do. I used to think I was the only one who was affected by what happened. But the more I get to know him, the more I suspect he was deeply affected, too. Only he won't admit it."

"Do you ever talk about it?"

Caroline's answer was swift and firm. "No! There's no point in it. We can't change what happened twenty-five years ago. That subject is like Pandora's box. Once we open it, we're both lost."

"But if you continue to be involved with him, at some point Marina will have to meet him," Marcia pointed out gently.

"I know. Believe me, I've thought of that. She'll be home for Thanksgiving." She shrugged. "Who knows? Maybe we won't be involved much longer. Every time we're together, I think it may be our last time."

"In a way, you want it to end, don't you?"

"Yes. But..."

She couldn't complete the thought, couldn't put into words her intense attraction to Rafe. When they were apart, it was easy to think it would be better if their relationship were to end. But when they were together all she was aware of was the touch and taste and feel of him. She was overwhelmed by the knowledge that no other man had ever affected her as he did. And no other man ever would.

The next evening Rafe took Caroline to his partner, Jim's, house for dinner. Jim and his wife Ginny had been pestering him for some time about meeting his new "lady love," and he had finally given in. Though he'd tried to tell himself that it didn't mean anything, he knew that wasn't true. Never before had he brought any of the women he was dating over to Jim and Ginny's house. This, he knew, was tacit acknowledgment that Caroline was different from the women he'd been involved with in the past.

"What a nice home," Caroline commented as they drove up.

"Yes, it is."

The house was nothing like Rafe's own. Relatively small, it was styled in the traditional Cape Cod design. It was very homey, complete with a white picket fence.

Rafe had barely rung the doorbell when the door was opened by both Jim and Ginny. Clearly, they'd been waiting eagerly for Rafe and Caroline's arrival.

As Rafe and Caroline entered the small foyer, Rafe made the introductions. Caroline's shyness was met by Jim and Ginny's effusiveness.

"It's about time Rafe brought you over," Ginny said in her usual forthright way. "We've been dying to meet you. Come on in to the living room with me, while the men make us each a drink. What'll you have?"

"White wine, if that's all right," Caroline answered.

"That's just fine. And I'll have the same," she said to Jim, before leading Caroline into the living room.

In deference to the cool late October evening, a fire was burning in the red brick fireplace. The decor of the room was unpretentious and old-fashioned—a chintz sofa and big, overstuffed armchairs, rugged oak tables and lots of plants. Rafe always felt at ease here. He was more relaxed and less guarded here than anywhere.

As he brought Caroline's glass of wine to her, he was struck by the similarity between her and Ginny. Both were brown-eyed blondes. And while Ginny was more of an extrovert, there was a gentleness about her that reminded him of Caroline. For the first time it occurred to him that their resemblance might be one reason why he'd always been so fond of Ginny and had stepped in to protect her when it looked like Jim might do something stupid that would hurt her and possibly break up their marriage.

Shifting his attention back to Caroline, he was struck by how well she fit in there. He couldn't envision Gayle Gillespie in the quiet setting, but it suited Caroline perfectly.

Motioning toward the photos on the mantel, Caroline asked Ginny, "Your children?"

"Yes, all three of the little devils. And another on the way."

"Congratulations."

"Thanks." Flashing a grin at Jim, she finished, "We're pretty happy about it."

"You must have your hands full with three boys."

"Well, there's never a dull moment. Just today one of 'em took it into his little six-year-old head to climb onto the roof. At the same time, the eight-year-old went into the attic. They were playing a game they made up called 'getaway kids.' Apparently, in this game they pretend to be kids who have escaped from some villain and are hiding out. Anyway, I didn't know who to get down first.

And while I was trying to figure it out, the three-year-old stubbed his toe and was screaming bloody murder!"

Jim interjected, "That was about the time you called me at the office and said you'd really appreciate it if I could come home fast."

Ginny smiled ruefully. "Jim's being polite. The truth is, I told him if he ever went into the office again on a Saturday, especially when I was expecting guests for dinner, I'd kill him."

"Now, honey, you know I'm really busy on this Shaw Avenue building."

"All I hear about is that building. I suppose Rafe's bored you to tears about it, too?"

Caroline nodded. "Well, yes, he told me about it."

"It's not exactly another run-of-the-mill project," Jim added defensively. "By the way, Rafe, some things came up today I wanted to discuss with you."

He and Rafe quickly got into a conversation that excluded the women. In response, Ginny invited Caroline to come into the kitchen with her while she made the final preparations for dinner.

"Can I help with anything?" Caroline offered.

"No, thanks. It's all done. I just wanted to get away from that business talk. The men are terrible about it."

Taking the lid off a pot on the stove, Ginny glanced at it quickly, then covered it again. "Five more minutes and the rice will be ready. Then we can eat. Everything else is already on the table. Let's sit down here in the breakfast nook while we wait for it."

"Where are your boys?" Caroline asked.

"At their grandparents for the weekend. My mom and dad picked them up about an hour ago. They live on a ranch over on the West Side and the boys just love visiting them. And God knows much as I love the little devils, it's great to get a break occasionally. Do you have any children?''

"Yes, a daughter. But she's grown.''

"I'm hoping this will be a girl. I'm sure they must be easier than boys.''

Caroline smiled. "I'm not so sure. I remember Marina doing some pretty crazy things. And when she got old enough to date, I worried about her a lot, in a way that I don't think I would have worried about a son. Now that she's out of college and on her own, I don't seem to worry quite so much.''

Surprise lit Ginny's dark eyes. "I can't believe you have a daughter out of college. You look younger than me, and I'm thirty-five.''

"Thanks for the compliment. But I'm Rafe's age. We went to high school together.''

"So that's where you met. I wondered, but I didn't want to seem too nosy. Jim told me in no uncertain terms not to cross-examine you. But, to be quite honest, I'm dying of curiosity. I care a lot about Rafe. He's so sweet.''

Sweet? There were a lot of words that described Rafael Marin, but sweet wasn't one of them, Caroline thought wryly.

Ginny went on, "So naturally I'm interested in someone he's obviously serious about.''

Serious about. Caroline was struck by the phrase. What had Rafe said or done that made Ginny think he was serious about her?

Ginny added, "Rafe mentioned that you moved to town recently. Was that when you met again?''

Caroline nodded. "We hadn't seen each other at all since high school.''

"How romantic!''

Just then Rafe and Jim came into the kitchen, interrupting the tête à tête.

"Hey, why'd you two leave?" Jim asked.

Ginny grimaced. "Maybe because we don't find construction talk all that fascinating."

"Okay, we can take a hint. No more shoptalk. I'm starving. Is dinner ready?"

"Yup."

Ginny rose and took the rice off the stove, putting it into a silver chafing dish. Then they all went into the dining room where the table was set exquisitely with china, crystal, silver and pristine white linen.

"This is lovely, Ginny," Caroline said sincerely.

"Thank you. It's a treat to be able to use our good stuff. With the boys, we don't dare do this. Now you and Rafe sit there, and Jim and I will sit here."

The meal was delicious, the company pleasant. Caroline liked both Jim and Ginny a lot and thought how nice it would be to see more of them. They were the kind of people with whom she was sure she could eventually become good friends.

If she continued seeing Rafe, she reminded herself.

After dinner, they had coffee in the living room, and Ginny asked lots of questions about The Dollhouse.

"If you have a girl, I'll give you one," Caroline responded generously.

Ginny blushed furiously. "Oh, dear, I wasn't fishing for a freebie, honest!"

Caroline smiled. "I know."

Ginny went on, "I'll bet your daughter has quite a collection."

Rafe felt stunned amazement. Shooting a quick look at Caroline, he saw her concentrating on her coffee, her eyes carefully averted from his.

"Yes," she murmured, without elaborating.

Forcing himself to sound calm, he interrupted, "It's getting late and we'd better be going. Ginny, the dinner was wonderful, as always."

Putting down his cup, he rose, forcing Caroline to do the same or look awkward.

"Well, I'm sorry you two have to rush off," Ginny responded. "It's been such an enjoyable evening." Turning to Caroline, she said meaningfully, "I hope we see you again real soon."

Caroline smiled in response, but said nothing. Clearly, she sensed what was bothering Rafe and knew they were in for a confrontation as soon as they were alone.

Neither said a thing as they got into the car, but the second they pulled out of the driveway Rafe began curtly, "So you have a daughter."

Caroline nodded.

"You never mentioned it to me."

Her face was set, her voice deceptively even. "The subject never came up."

"Actually, I believe it did, at the reunion."

Neither had ever referred to that tumultuous night because it was such a sensitive subject. The fact that Rafe did so now was proof of his anger.

He went on in a voice as cold as ice, "Any other offspring you haven't seen fit to mention?"

"No."

She turned to face him angrily. He kept his eyes on the road and didn't meet her look. "I didn't say anything about her because I didn't think you'd be interested."

Right. Why should he be interested in Edward's child? he asked himself bitterly. But he knew the answer all too well. He was interested because Caroline had given up his own child, only to go on and have another with someone else.

Blind rage filled him. The acute sense of loss that he'd lived with every day for twenty-five years was suddenly more than he could bear. Turning the car sharply into Caroline's driveway with a squeal of tires, he brought it to a jerky stop.

"Rafe..."

Caroline's voice was tentative, hurt, confused.

But he was too caught up in his own pain to deal with hers.

Getting out, he slammed the door, then went around to open hers. He didn't offer her his hand, as he usually did, but simply stood there while she got out. Then he slammed shut that door also. And without saying a word to her, he went back to the driver's side, got in and roared off, leaving her standing there with an anguished expression on her face.

He took deserted back roads to his house because he was in no mood to deal with the slower city traffic. The silver Jaguar sped through the black autumn night like a streak of lightning. At the wheel, Rafe was barely aware of his surroundings. He kept thinking over and over again, *She gave up my child and kept Edward's.*

The thought was like a stiletto, twisting and turning in his gut.

He sped up the road that wound around the hill to his house, taking the corners much too fast. At that point he wouldn't have cared if the car had gone sailing off into the night.

When he reached his house, he walked through it without bothering to turn on the lights. In his study, he turned on the small desk lamp, then taking a small key from his key ring he unlocked the bottom desk drawer.

The drawer was empty save for one book. The thin volume was dusty. It had sat in that drawer, undisturbed, since Rafe had bought the desk ten years earlier.

Now, Rafe picked it up. The title, *Sonnets From the Portuguese,* was illuminated for a second in the dim lamplight. Then Rafe quickly opened it and took out a slip of paper pressed between the pages. The paper had yellowed with age, but the writing was still perfectly legible.

Like a masochist reveling in his misery, Rafe reread the brief note:

Rafe, My parents have made arrangements for me to stay at a home for unwed mothers. I will give the baby up for adoption. It is for the best. Keeping a little half-breed would ruin my life. You've hurt me enough—I don't ever want to see you again.

                                                    Caroline

Rafe had last read the note twenty-five years earlier, but its impact on him now was almost as powerful. His hand holding it shook, and unshed tears filled his eyes.

You've hurt me enough.

Maybe he had, unintentionally. But she'd hurt him just as much. Not a day had gone by that he hadn't wondered where she was, what she was doing. And where their child was and if it was all right. The thought that it might be in pain, might need its father, was more than he could stand to think of.

He had always prided himself on his strength of will, his toughness. The Clovis establishment hadn't been able to bring him to his knees. But Caroline had.

He still remembered the utter humiliation he had felt when he'd gone to her father, asking him to let them marry. Her father had given him the note, saying, "Caroline's come to her senses. Read this. And then go back to your own kind. You've done enough damage around here."

His own father had cautioned him to forget the girl. Getting mixed up with a family as influential as hers could only cause problems. Implicit in his words was the unspoken conviction that the Marins weren't good enough for the Cummings.

Rafe had sworn that that kind of pain and humiliation would never happen again. Then, when he learned of her child, it *did* happen.

Slowly, he put the note back inside the book and closed the cover. After putting the book back into the drawer, he locked it once more.

During the three months he'd been involved with Caroline, he'd become more and more reluctant to go through with his plan of revenge. He was falling in love with her all over again, despite his determination not to let that happen. The old magic was still there, even stronger, in fact.

At first he was simply attracted to her physically. She stirred his blood as no other woman had ever done. And when he was in her arms, he ceased to think, to remember what she had done to him. All he was aware of then was her softness, her passion, her sweetness.

Then as he got to know her, to learn what kind of woman she had grown into, he was filled with a grudging admiration for her. She was bright and strong and fiercely independent. And he loved her even more than he had when she was a naive girl.

But now . . . now that was finished. Over. He felt nothing for her but anger. He would go through with his plan. All he had to do now was get past that final barrier she still retained. He had to make her face the fact that she loved him, and he had to make her admit it to him.

All during that last week in October, business improved radically. The advertisement about special orders for Christmas brought in many people. That, on top of the charity auction, made The Dollhouse a success at last.

On Friday after work, Marcia and Caroline opened a bottle of champagne to celebrate signing a new, one year lease.

Holding up her glass, Marcia said happily, "Here's to The Dollhouse. May it be in business forever!"

Caroline touched her glass against Marcia's, then took a small sip of the sparkling golden liquid.

Putting down her glass, Marcia went on in a no-nonsense tone, "All right, out with it. What's wrong?"

"Nothing's wrong. We're a success." Caroline tried to sound happy, but her voice lacked conviction.

"I know we're a success. I'm thrilled about it. But you're not. Judging from the way you look, anyone would think we were going out of business. You've looked this way all week. I thought you were just concerned about whether or not we were going to make it. But now that it's definite that we are, you still look miserable."

Caroline couldn't keep it inside any longer. Hesitantly, barely holding back the tears, she related the big blowup with Rafe.

"But why was he so angry that you hadn't told him about Marina?" Marcia asked.

"I don't know. God, I'm so confused."

"Carrie, are you sure he wasn't interested in knowing about her?"

"He never once asked about her. I honestly don't think it's that."

"Maybe he was just waiting for you to make the first move, so to speak. To bring up the subject and give him an opening to ask about her."

"Rafe isn't usually reticent about going after what he wants," Caroline responded dryly.

"Wait a minute! Carrie, Rafe never knew you had—a boy or a girl, did he?"

Caroline shook her head.

"Maybe that's it! It was the first time he learned what your child was, and it really shook him. It was probably easier for him not to think about her when he didn't even know if she was a girl or a boy."

"Maybe. Oh, hell, I don't know what came over him. I only know I've never seen him that angry."

"Did you try to call him, to talk about it?"

Caroline shook her head. "I . . . I couldn't do that."

"Caroline Turner, you coward! Remember all that advice you gave me not a month ago about times being different now than when we were seventeen, and we have to go after what we want?"

Caroline smiled sheepishly. "I know. But it's easier to give advice like that than it is to take it."

"Well, I'm giving you the same advice right now. Call him. Whatever happens, you can't become any more miserable than you are right now."

"I'll think about it."

"Carrie . . ."

"That's all I can do right now, Marcia."

"Okay, I won't push you. But think about it very seriously. You refused to give up where this business is concerned. Use some of that same tenacity on Rafe."

But as Caroline walked into her house that evening, she wasn't at all sure she could screw up the courage to call Rafe. She couldn't get over how angry he'd been. She didn't understand his reaction to her mentioning their child, but she knew one thing—he felt very strongly about it. Whatever was going on emotionally with him, it was something only he could resolve.

She paused to start a small fire in the fireplace, for the night was chilly. In her bedroom, she took off her work clothes and was about to slip on jeans and a sweater when the doorbell rang. Throwing on a white satin robe, she pulled the sash tight as she went to the door. She knew that it was undoubtedly Marcia, probably with Jack, coming over to cheer her up. But when she opened the door, she found Rafe standing there.

Not saying a word, he took her in his arms and kissed her hungrily.

Without thinking, moved by pure instinct, she responded, giving herself up completely to his searing kiss. She felt like a drowning woman who had suddenly been thrown a lifeline.

When they finally pulled apart, he whispered hoarsely, "I'm sorry. I'm so sorry..."

"Hush, now, it's all right, sweetheart."

Kicking the door closed behind him, he picked her up and carried her over to the rug in front of the fireplace. It only took seconds for her robe and his clothes to be discarded. Then they were on the soft white rug, and nothing mattered but the feel of each other, the satisfying of the terrible emptiness that had gripped both of them for six long days and nights.

He murmured her name over and over again, "Caroline, my Caroline. My God, how I've missed you!"

Her body molded instinctively to his. Her hands slid to the nape of his neck, her fingers twining through his black hair. Her lips parted as she opened up to his probing tongue. As his tongue sought hers relentlessly, she responded fully to his rising passion.

When he pulled back to look down at her, she gazed up at him with all the love in the world shining in her golden eyes. She wanted him. And nothing else in the world mattered.

"It feels like a lifetime since I held you," he whispered, his voice shaken.

"I'm here now, in your arms. Love me, Rafe. Love me now."

Her supple body arched against him, adding exquisite sexual tension to her appeal.

For an instant his muscles tensed beneath her fingertips. His gray eyes slid over her slender body. The fire in his gaze sent her entire body tingling with feverish anticipation.

The utter maleness of him—his strong, lithe body, the rippling muscles across his shoulders, his flat stomach and sinewy thighs—caused her breath to catch in her throat.

Slowly, with all the gentleness he could muster, he joined with her, pressing his own naked skin against hers. His dark skin glistened in the pale light of the one lamp that was burning in the room. Her own skin was pale against his.

But each wanted the other too desperately to go slowly. They clung to each other, saying nothing, yet by their movements urging each other on to greater heights of passion. Then, after what seemed only moments, they shuddered against each other, as the tremendous tension that had built up between them burst in a joy so profound it left their hearts and minds reeling.

Afterwards, Rafe continued to hold Caroline against him, whispering words that were unintelligible but clearly heartfelt and loving. Her arms were still around him, reluctant to ever let go.

I love him, she thought, over and over.

She knew that someday, soon, she would have to tell him so.

Chapter Thirteen

November dawned cold and rainy. "An early winter," people said, shaking their heads. It was bad news for the orange growers, who had to worry about killing frosts.

In The Dollhouse, Marcia and Caroline worked feverishly to handle the special orders for Christmas that came pouring in every day. They hired a part-time sales clerk to help in the shop and several Hmong seamstresses to help make the dolls.

Jack gave Marcia an engagement ring and they made plans for a spring wedding. Marcia was absolutely beaming. Her happiness could hardly be contained. She talked excitedly of the plans for the wedding as if she were a first time bride of twenty.

"Just a small ceremony in The Church of the Wayfarer in Carmel," she told Caroline. "Only close friends and family. Oh, Carrie, you will be my maid of honor, won't you?"

Caroline laughed. "Of course. Now that's something I haven't done in years."

"We're going to honeymoon in Carmel."

"Oh, Marcia, it sounds heavenly. Have you told Jason and Jill?"

Marcia nodded. "That was the only hard part. I was so afraid they would resent Jack. They adored Carl, you know. But they both came home from school last weekend especially to meet him, and they got along great."

"I'm not surprised. Jack is awfully nice."

"Carrie, you should have heard him. He told them he wouldn't try to take their father's place, he just wanted to be their friend. He said he hoped they would approve because it would make me unhappy if they didn't, and my happiness was the most important thing to him. Then he told them he loved me very much and would do everything he could to make me glad I'd married him. Well, how could they resent him after that?"

"Marcia, that's wonderful. Jack is a very special man."

"Don't I know it!"

"Where will you live, your house or his?"

"We're going to sell both of them and buy a new place. After all, this is a new start for both of us."

"Oh, I'm glad you're making a new start. You have so much of your life left to live."

Marcia's broad smile slowly faded and she grew thoughtful. Finally, she said carefully, "You know, Carrie, it wasn't that long ago that the good times seemed to be over for both of us. I was a widow, with nothing to look forward to but a boring job and dusting a big, empty house. When I thought of Jason and Jill leaving for college, I felt absolute panic."

"I know. But you didn't let them see that. And I admire you so much for not burdening them with your fear."

"Well, I admire the way you didn't give in to depression when Edward left. You were so strong. But I know you must have been terrified of the thought of having to put your life back together at a time when you'd probably expected to have security."

"Oh, I was terrified, all right. There was so much to handle—Edward's rejection, the sense of failure with the divorce, the panic at being on my own at a time when I had expected to be settled. The worst of it was trying to figure out how I was going to support myself. When I looked at the other women in the job market, young women with college degrees, I felt so useless. And as for men and dating, well, I had no illusions about the competition there. Why should any man want me when he could have a nubile twenty-year-old?"

Marcia laughed softly. "I know. I felt the same way. I just assumed that romance was a thing of my youth, something I would never have a shot at again."

"Forty was the magic number. When we both passed that, in a sense the best part of life seemed to be over."

"*Seemed* to be is right. And why? Because they say so—whoever they are. You'd think we were expected to roll over and play dead."

Caroline grinned. "Well, we haven't done that."

"You bet we haven't. Look at us! In our prime, better than we've ever been, without the insecurity and inexperience of our twenties, or the child rearing responsibilities that kept us tied down in our thirties. We're free to be whatever we damn well choose."

"You're right. I feel stronger than ever. Maybe women don't come of age until their forties."

"Carrie, that's got to be true. We live so long now, we can pack two lives into one. I had one kind of life with Carl—a wonderful, fulfilling life—and now I intend to have another kind of life with this shop and with Jack. I'm starting something brand new and I'm so excited I can hardly stand it!"

Caroline laughed happily. "Oh, I know exactly how you feel. Since things have worked out with this shop, and especially since I've stopped fighting what I feel for Rafe, I feel like life is more exciting now than it's ever been. Maybe forty is the beginning, not the beginning of the end."

Marcia grinned wickedly. "You know, we sound just like Joan Collins."

Caroline's laughter was warm with delight. "Why not?"

Just then the phone rang, interrupting their conversation. At almost the same moment a customer came in. While Marcia answered the phone, Caroline waited on the customer, all the while feeling euphoria bubbling up inside her. Life was turning out okay after all. And the best part of it was Rafe.

She saw him nearly every day. Things were wonderful between them, and there was no repeat of the awful episode when he had learned about Marina and gotten so angry. Caroline began to think about how she was going to break the news to Marina that she was dating Rafe. And she had an endless interior dialogue with herself, arguing back and forth about whether she should tell Marina the truth—that Rafe, not Edward, was Marina's father.

Edward had legally adopted Marina when she was only two years old and had been more than willing to raise the child as his own. Because of Edward and Caroline's agreement to protect Marina by lying about their wedding date, Marina had no suspicion that Edward wasn't her father. Even though Marina and Edward hadn't been very close, she was devastated by her parents' divorce and Edward's immediate remarriage to another woman.

But Caroline knew that Marina might very well be even more devastated to learn that the man she had always thought of as her father, wasn't. And a man she'd never met, was. She realized that she would have to reach some sort of a decision soon, for Marina would be home for Thanksgiving and would meet Rafe then.

One day she was thinking about this problem, and at the same time working on a doll, when the telephone on the small desk in the workroom rang. Picking it up, she answered distractedly, "The Dollhouse."

"Caroline, is that you?"

"Yes. Who is this?"

"Jim, Rafe's partner."

His voice was so strained, Caroline immediately sensed that something was wrong. She gripped the receiver just a little more firmly and asked nervously, "Yes, Jim, what is it?"

"Caroline, Rafe's been injured."

"Oh, my God! What happened? Is he all right?"

"I don't know what to tell you. I'm at the hospital, waiting to talk to the doctor. I'm not sure of the extent of his injuries."

"Where is he?"

"St. Agnes Hospital."

"I'll be right there."

She hung up, at the same time grabbing her purse from on top a nearby file cabinet. Pausing only long enough to tell Marcia what had happened, she left hurriedly. The drive across town to St. Agnes would normally have taken twenty minutes. Caroline made it in ten.

She hurried through the entrance doors up to the information desk. There she learned that Rafe was in Room 420. A moment later she arrived outside the room to find a No Visitors sign hanging on the door.

She stood there, a lump in her throat and her knees weak. All she could think of was "I never told him I love him."

"Caroline!"

Turning, she found Jim walking toward her.

When he reached her, he hugged her warmly, then, putting one arm around her shoulder, led her to some nearby chairs. As they sat down, she asked anxiously, "How bad is it?"

"He'll be okay. Don't worry. I just talked to the doctor and he said there's a slight concussion, some slight cuts and bruises and a bad gash on his forehead. If it weren't for the concussion, they would have simply treated him and released him. But the doctor wants to keep an eye on him for a while. Concussions can be tricky."

Caroline began to cry from sheer relief.

Wrapping his arms around her, Jim murmured, "It's all right. He's going to be okay. Rafe's damn tough."

Brushing the tears from her pale cheeks, she asked, "But what happened?"

"We were looking over the Shaw Avenue building. Rafe likes to get up on the scaffolding and inspect things personally."

She nodded. "Yes, I know. He told me once. Did he fall?"

"Yes. Fortunately, a pile of sawdust broke the fall, or he would be a lot worse off than he is." Jim shook his head. "I don't know what came over him today. Normally, he has the balance of a cat. I guess his mind wandered for a second, and that was all it took."

"Can I see him?"

"I'm afraid not. The doctor gave him a pretty strong painkiller and it knocked him out."

"Oh, Jim, while I was driving over here all sorts of awful thoughts kept going through my head."

She began to cry again, hating herself for her weakness but unable to stop.

"It's all right, Caroline, let it all out. I can imagine what you went through. I felt the same way. I saw him fall, and when I rushed over to him I didn't know if he'd still be breathing or not."

Looking at him, Caroline saw lines of strain on his normally happy countenance.

"Can I take a quick look, just . . . just to make sure?" she asked.

He smiled. "Sure. Come on."

He led her to the door and she stepped inside quietly. Only a dim light near the bed relieved the darkness of the room. Rafe lay there under a white sheet, wearing a hospital gown. There were several small bandages on his arms and a large one on his forehead. His face was pale but there was so sign of strain as he slept heavily.

Gazing at him, Caroline's heart swelled with love. She wanted to stroke his face and murmur words of love.

What a fool I've been, she thought. *I've always loved him. I always will. It's time I told him.*

As soon as he awoke, she intended to do just that.

Caroline was at the hospital the next afternoon, the minute that visiting hours began. When she walked into Rafe's room, she found him dressed and ready to check out. He smiled sheepishly when he saw her, and she sensed that he was embarrassed somehow.

"I guess Jim told you," he said.

She nodded.

"I made a damn fool of myself."

"Don't go all macho and ridiculous. Are you sure you should be leaving already?"

"Positive. I'm fine, except for the worst headache I can ever remember having. I was just getting ready to call Jim and see if he'd drive me home."

"I'll do it, if you'd like."

"Are you sure you can be away from the shop?"

"Yes. Marcia can handle it for the rest of the afternoon."

"Then let's blow this joint," he said with a grin. "Hospitals aren't my favorite places."

A few minutes later they were driving toward his house. Rafe was still a little more pale than usual, and his entire body was sore, but otherwise, he said, he was fine.

As she stopped in front of his house, Caroline thought that it seemed like a long time since she'd last been there. She smiled as she remembered the night when they had been more interested in making love than eating dinner, and the raccoon had taken care of the food for them.

At that time she was still telling herself that all she felt for him was a strong physical attraction. She had admitted the truth to herself since then. It was time to admit it to him.

She had no idea how he would react. She sensed that he loved her, too. If she was wrong... well, she would have to deal with that somehow. But surely she wasn't wrong, she told herself. He couldn't make love to her as he did without feeling love for her.

All of this went through her head as she saw him into the house. When he was comfortably settled in a chair in the living room, she knelt by his knees and looked up at him.

"I love you," she said simply.

The brief words were uttered so quietly that for a moment he didn't behave as if he'd heard. But she knew that he must have. She waited...waited for him to say, "I love you, too."

When he finally spoke, the words weren't what she'd expected or hoped. "Caroline, are you sure?"

She nodded.

He leaned down to look intently into her eyes. "You said you didn't want to love me."

"I didn't. I fought it. But when we were apart for that week, I realized how much you meant to me. I knew then it was only a matter of time before I would tell you. Then, when I heard that you were hurt, and I thought that I might lose you . . . well, time ran out."

"You love me," he repeated slowly, as if he couldn't believe it. Almost as if he didn't want to believe it.

Whatever response she had expected from him, it wasn't this. As he leaned back in his chair and stared past her, out the window, she wondered what he was thinking, and especially what he was feeling. Was he glad she loved him? Or was he concerned that she might expect more from their relationship now? Had it been purely physical, as far as he was concerned?

She had declared her love for him with complete confidence that it would at the very least please him. Now that confidence began to waver.

She took his hands in hers and clasped them tightly. "Rafe, I'm not asking you to love me." Her full mouth curved in a rueful smile. "I know you don't want to, any more than I wanted to love you. But I had to tell you how I feel. I couldn't keep it inside."

He looked down at her. "And the past?"

"Is dead and buried. I don't want to spend the rest of my life fighting what I feel for you because of something that happened between us twenty-five years ago. It's such a waste. And life is too short, too precious, to waste a single moment, let alone year after bitter year."

He closed his eyes and sighed heavily. Though he didn't take his hands from hers, she could feel him slipping away from her. She didn't know why or how, she only knew it was happening.

A sense of desperation welled up deep inside her. She wanted to pull him back, to feel close to him again. Only her pride kept her from begging him not to slip away from her.

"Rafe..."

He opened his eyes and looked down at her. The expression in his eyes was unfathomable. But somehow Caroline sensed that both pity and anger warred within him.

He went on slowly, "I'm sorry if I seem out of it. They gave me another painkiller today just before I left, and I feel lightheaded."

"Of course," she whispered. "I should have realized you've had a rough time and are in no shape for a heavy discussion. What would you like me to do?"

"I really need to rest. Do you mind?"

"No, of course not."

She let go of his hands and rose. Bending down to kiss his forehead, she said, "If there's anything I can do, call me. Goodbye, love."

His response was a barely audible whisper. "Goodbye."

As Caroline drove away a moment later, she felt strangely unsettled. She told herself that Rafe was tired and hurt and not clearheaded. Yet somehow all of those obvious facts didn't make her feel better. She didn't for one moment regret telling him of her love. And yet she couldn't shake off the feeling that something was very wrong.

That night Rafe lay in bed in the darkness. It was raining and he could hear the staccato patter of the rain against the window. But it wasn't the rain or the wind moaning around the house that kept him awake. He couldn't stop thinking of Caroline.

I love you, she'd said. Her voice, her eyes, the way she held herself declared it to be true. She offered her heart to him with no strings attached, nothing held back. She was his. Finally, after all the long, lonely years, she was his.

He should be glad. Triumphant. He had achieved his goal of making her care for him again. Now the only thing left to do was to walk out on her.

And he knew exactly how he was going to do it. They were supposed to go up to Jim and Ginny's cabin at Shaver Lake on Saturday. The plan was for him to pick up Caroline at her house at nine in the morning. She would be packed and ready to have a wonderful weekend.

The last thing in the world she would be expecting would be for him to tell her he was never going to see her again. But that was exactly what he was going to do.

On Saturday morning, Caroline rose early. She packed a small overnight bag with the essentials for a one-night trip, then dressed in cream-colored corduroy slacks, a cream-and-blue plaid blouse and comfortable walking boots. Across her bag she laid a heavy sheepskin jacket. It would be cold up in the mountains.

She was excited about the trip, but a little nervous as well. She hadn't seen Rafe in several days, not since she'd driven him home after his brief stay in the hospital. They'd talked on the phone once, but he had said he wasn't feeling up to going out.

She couldn't help wondering if that was just an excuse to avoid her because he'd been put off by her declaration of love. But if so, surely he would have shelved their plans for this weekend in the mountains?

As she pulled her hair back in a ponytail and applied a dash of gold powder to her eyelids and gloss to her lips, she told herself she was being ridiculous.

When the doorbell rang, she answered it quickly. She greeted Rafe with her most dazzling smile.

"You're right on time. Fortunately, so am I," she said breezily. "I'm really excited about this. We've been so busy at the shop, I've been working around the clock. It will be wonderful to have a whole weekend to relax."

Giving him a meaningful look, she finished, "And to spend it with you. Much as I like Jim and Ginny, I have to admit I'm glad we're going to have the place to ourselves."

She smiled up at him, her expression warm and happy and almost heartbreakingly trusting. For one split second Rafe seemed to hold his breath, as one does before taking a big plunge.

Caroline's brown eyes met his gray ones. Something she saw in them seemed to check her excitement and her smile wavered just a little.

And then he spoke.

"We're not going."

She waited for something more, an explanation. When it didn't come, she said slowly, "Oh . . . I see. What happened?"

His voice was flat, even, almost devoid of emotion. "Nothing happened. But we're not going. And I won't be seeing you again."

Her thick golden lashes fluttered in surprise. Her lips parted slightly as she caught her breath. Tears stung the corners of her eyes, and she fought them back.

She opened her mouth to speak, stopped, then began again in a quavering tone that betrayed her shock. "What do you mean, Rafe?"

He couldn't meet her look. Instead, he looked past her, and answered curtly, "It's clear enough, isn't it? I don't want to see you again. I thought it would be better to tell you in person than to simply stop calling you."

Her lips curved slightly in a wistful smile. "Yes, that's certainly thoughtful of you. It would have been rather humiliating to be left dangling, wondering what happened. By the way, do you mind if I ask what *did* happen?"

"I never wanted a serious relationship with you, Caroline. You knew that."

"I knew that. But I thought . . . that is, you seemed to care for me as much as I care for you."

"Obviously, you were wrong."

"Obviously."

He stood there for a moment, looking awkward and tense. Then, with a curt, "Goodbye," he turned on his heel and headed out the door.

Suddenly the reality of what was happening sank into Caroline's numb mind. Rafe was leaving. Forever. He wasn't angry. This wasn't a snit. He was quite serious.

"Wait!"

He stopped just inside the door, but didn't turn around.

"What?"

"Rafe, I don't believe this is happening. It's all wrong somehow."

Walking over to him, she put her hands on his shoulders and turned him to face her. "I love you. And I can't have misjudged your feelings for me so completely. I just know I can't."

His face was set, his entire body rigid beneath her touch.

"We enjoyed each other for a while, but that's all it was. And it *is* over."

She stepped back as if he'd struck her. She was absolutely shattered. She loved him and he was walking out of her life forever. The cold, hard feeling that was beginning to fill her was worse than anything she had ever imagined.

Her innate pride forbade her to beg. She wouldn't crumble in front of him. Whatever happened after he was gone, she wouldn't let him see her fall apart now. Fighting back tears, her head held determinedly high, she watched silently as he turned and walked out the door.

When he had gone, the tears coursed freely down her pale cheeks. She didn't even try to stop them, to get hold of herself for several minutes. Her slender body was racked by sobs as she curled up in a chair, hugging herself tightly.

She didn't understand what had just happened. Or why. But she knew if she stayed in her house, crying, she would be lost. Drying her eyes on her sleeve, she picked up the small suitcase and her jacket and took them out to her car. Tossing them in the backseat, she got in and drove to the shop. It was only nine-thirty, not quite time to open yet, but she knew Marcia would be there, getting ready for a busy Saturday.

When she got to the shopping center, she parked in an empty space directly in front of the shop. Inside, she saw Marcia counting the money in the cash register. Going up to the door, she knocked on it lightly.

Glancing up, Marcia looked surprised to see her. Hurrying to the door, she unlocked it and said cheerfully, "Why, Carrie, I thought you'd be gone by now. Are you leaving later?"

"I'm not going," she said in a voice barely above a whisper as she entered the shop.

"Wait a minute, you look awful. What happened?"

Caroline's bottom lip trembled, but she managed to keep from crying as she briefly explained the scene with Rafe.

"The bastard!" Marcia said furiously. "How dare he do this to you again!"

Caroline's smile was bitter. "Yes...again. You'd think once would have been enough for me, but apparently I'm a slow learner where Rafael Marin is concerned."

Marcia threw her arms around Caroline and hugged her reassuringly. "Oh, Carrie, I'm so sorry. So very sorry."

"Marcia, I came to tell you that I've got to get away for a while. Just a few days..."

"Of course you do. And for heaven's sakes, don't worry about coming back for a long time. Lisa and I can hold down the fort and the dolls you're working on can just wait."

"Marcia, thanks for understanding. I won't stay away long, though. I promise."

"Where will you be in case I need to get in touch with you?"

Caroline hadn't thought where she would go. She only knew she couldn't stay in the same town with Rafe. Thinking furiously, she quickly decided against San Francisco, which she still associated with Edward, and Big Sur. Actually, she would have liked nothing better than to see Marina, but she knew there was no way she could see her without giving away what had happened. And that she didn't want to do.

Suddenly, she remembered a place she'd gone to once. A small, quiet, peaceful place where no one knew her, and she knew no one. A place where she could grieve in private and begin to mend her broken heart.

Looking at Marcia, she said, "I'm going to Mendocino."

"That little fishing village on the coast of Northern California?"

"Yes. There's a small inn up there called The Seagull. It shouldn't be crowded at this time of year. I'll be there."

"Okay. Call me when you get there. I'll be worried until I hear you're okay."

"I'm not okay now, but I will be. Bye, Marcia."

Marcia hugged her one last time, then watched sadly as she went outside and drove away.

On the other side of town, Rafe drove toward his office in downtown Fresno. He would get some work done. That would take his mind off the turmoil going on inside him. There were some cost overruns on the Shaw Avenue project that needed attention.

Yet as he maneuvered his car through the streets crowded with weekend shoppers, he couldn't get the scene out of his mind. He should feel triumphant, he knew. He'd achieved his goal of revenge.

But to his chagrin, it wasn't sweet. In fact, it was downright bitter.

He knew that for the rest of his life he would remember how Caroline had looked—stunned, yet bravely refusing to give way to the humiliation and pain she must be feeling. She had never looked lovelier, had never affected him more profoundly.

And he had never loved her more.

Suddenly, the car in front of him stopped for a pedestrian. Slamming on his brakes, Rafe hit his horn and cursed the other driver.

The driver turned and gave him an angry "What are you upset for, anyway?" look. When he moved forward again, it was with deliberate slowness.

Rafe's unwarranted anger was gone as soon as it had come. He sat there, not moving, his mind reeling.

He loved her.

He had refused to even think those words up till now. But he could no longer avoid them. She was the only woman he'd ever loved. She was the reason why he'd never married. She had made him feel more of a man than all the Gayles he'd known over a lot of years. The only time his house seemed like a home was when she was in it with him.

He had lived all those years without her, driven by bitterness, and where had it gotten him? He was nothing without her.

Revenge hadn't worked. Maybe it was time to try forgiveness.

A car pulled up behind him and the driver leaned irately on his horn. Looking up sharply, Rafe realized that he was stopped in the middle of the street. Taking his foot off the brake, he moved on, but as soon as possible he turned and headed back the way he'd come.

Back to Caroline.

When he got to her house he saw that her car was gone. With a sinking feeling, he ran up to her door and pounded on it heavily, shouting her name. But it was too late.

Caroline was gone.

Chapter Fourteen

Three days passed. During those three seemingly end-less days, Rafe was in hell. He practically camped out at Caroline's house, but she didn't return. And Marcia, who told him in no uncertain terms what she thought of him, refused to tell him where Caroline had gone.

He didn't go to work on Monday, but on Tuesday he had an important meeting that he couldn't miss. On his way to the office he stopped by Caroline's house—just in case. She had to come back sometime, he reasoned, and he intended to keep going by her house until she finally returned.

As he pulled up in front of her house, he saw an ancient, faded yellow Volkswagen convertible in the drive-way. A young woman was just taking a suitcase out of it.

Getting out of his car, Rafe hurried toward her.

"Excuse me, miss."

She turned, and for an instant it was like looking in a mirror...gray eyes in sharp contrast to black hair and an impudent tilt to the firm chin.

"Yes?"

"I...I'm a friend of Caroline Turner's. Are you by any chance her daughter?"

The pretty young woman smiled. She exuded a warmth that Rafe knew must have melted more than one young man's heart.

"Yes, I was going to surprise her by coming home early for Thanksgiving. But the surprise is on me. Mom's gone. It's a good thing she sent me a key to the house, or I'd be out in the cold, literally."

"I was aware your mother was gone. I stopped by hoping she might have returned."

The young woman's eyes surveyed him critically, taking in the expensive suit, and behind him, the Jaguar. Apparently deciding he was all right, she smiled again, and asked, "Do you know where she went?"

"No, unfortunately she didn't mention where she was going or when she would return. Don't you know?"

She shook her head. "Nope. But when the shop opens at ten, I'll call her partner, Marcia. I'm sure she'll know. It's probably a business trip, anyway."

Suddenly remembering her manners, she put down her suitcase and held out a hand. "By the way, I'm Marina, what's your name?"

He stood thunderstruck. The moment he'd looked at her, he knew, but it seemed too fantastic to be true. This girl wasn't Edward's daughter. She was *his*. It was all so obvious—his coloring, even his name, *Marina*.

He took her hand and held it in his. His throat constricted and his eyes misted with tears as he looked at his daughter for the first time. Caroline hadn't given her up after all. Rafe had no idea what had happened twenty-five years earlier. But whatever had happened, she had kept his child.

"I asked your name," Marina repeated, taking her hand from his.

When he spoke it was a voice utterly unlike his own. "I'm sorry. It's . . . Rafael Marin."

She didn't recognize the name. Clearly, Caroline had told Marina nothing of him.

"I'm pleased to meet you, Mr. Marin."

Looking at her intently, he responded, "It's very nice meeting you, Marina."

"Well, I'd better get inside before I freeze. I'll tell Mom you stopped by."

"Yes. I'm sure I'll be seeing you again real soon. Goodbye, Marina."

Reluctantly, he tore himself away from his daughter. There was a great deal to say to her, but it would have to wait. First he had to find Caroline and somehow make up to her for what he'd done.

Hurrying back home, he called the office and told a surprised Jim he wouldn't be in.

"But the meeting . . ."

"You handle it. I've got something much more important to do. I'll call you when I get back."

"Get back? But where are you going?"

"I don't know yet. Jim, I've got to go. Bye."

Stopping only to take the book out of his desk drawer, he drove to The Dollhouse.

It wasn't quite ten o'clock and the door was still locked, but Rafe saw Marcia inside. When he knocked on the door, she looked at him angrily and motioned to him to go away. He shook his head no and pounded harder on the door.

Afraid the glass door would break, Marcia hurried over to unlock it.

"It's no use, Rafe, I'm not about to tell you anything about Caroline!"

He shoved the note into her hands. "Read this," he snapped.

She hesitated, and for an instant he was afraid she was going to rip the note in half and fling it in his face. But apparently thinking better of the impulse, she sighed angrily, then did as he ordered.

In a moment her startled eyes came back to his and her voice was confused. "What is this?"

"Caroline's father gave it to me twenty-five years ago, when I went to their house to ask if we could get married."

"But...this isn't the note Caroline wrote you. She would never have said these things."

"I know that now. What did she write, Marcia?"

Marcia hesitated, unsure if she should trust him.

"Please," he begged. "I have to know."

Then, when she still hesitated, he said heavily, "I met Marina. I met my *daughter*. My God, Marcia, I thought Caroline had given her up!"

"Oh, Rafe, I'm afraid you two have been living a tragedy. Here, come inside. I've got a lot to tell you."

She locked the door behind him, leaving up the Closed sign even though it was nearly ten o'clock. In the workroom, she poured them each a cup of strong, black coffee, then sat down facing him.

"What happened, Marcia?"

"Caroline's parents were furious, of course. They ordered her to go away somewhere and give the baby up for adoption. But she refused."

"Why didn't she tell me?"

"She tried to. She wrote a note, telling you that she would have to go away until her eighteenth birthday."

"Why?"

"Her father threatened to charge you with statutory rape. Once she turned eighteen, he would no longer have any authority over her. In her note, she told you she would come back to you then, if you wanted her to. She asked you to let her know if you wanted her to come back. When she didn't hear from you . . ."

Marcia's words trailed off, but the meaning was unmistakable.

Looking at her with a ragged, haunted expression on his face, Rafe said slowly, "I never got that note."

"But she gave it to your father to give to you."

Rafe thought back to what his father had said at that time. He remembered the fear on his father's face, fear for Rafe's welfare. And suddenly he knew what must have happened.

"I think my father probably gave the note to Mr. Cummings under the misguided impression it would save me from further trouble. He destroyed it and wrote this one."

"But couldn't you see it isn't Caroline's writing?"

"How could I know that? The only time I saw her writing was an inscription in a book. It simply didn't occur to me to question it."

Marcia's deep blue eyes softened as they looked at him. "And you were so hurt by what you thought she said in the note, that you didn't try to see her again."

He shook his head heavily.

"My God," Marcia whispered. "What they did to both of you."

"Marcia, what happened to her? Where did she go?"

"To San Francisco. To a home for unwed mothers. When Marina was born, Carrie supported her by working as a sales clerk at Macy's. It was very hard, because for a long time her parents wouldn't have anything to do with her. But she was strong. You should have seen them together. Carrie was eighteen and scared, but she didn't let it show. And she loved Marina so much."

Rafe's face contorted in anguish. "I would have given anything to be with her then."

"I know. Oh, Rafe, I know that now."

"She married Edward for Marina's sake, didn't she?"

Marcia nodded. "I think so. She would never admit it, but I know she didn't really love him."

"Where is she right now?"

When Marcia hesitated, he went on, "I'm not going to hurt her anymore. I'm going to try to make up to her for... for everything."

"All right. She's in Mendocino, on Highway 1 about 170 miles north of San Francisco. At a place called The Seagull Inn. I'm not sure when she's coming back."

He rose. "It doesn't matter. I'm going to her."

He strode out to his car and pointed it north.

Caroline walked along the sandy beach, her hands shoved in the pockets of her bulky sheepskin jacket. It was cold in Mendocino, especially on the beach where the wind coming in off the ocean was sharp. But the view was magnificent—emerald-green headlands stretched down to steep cliffs, then below them, sandy coves. In the water, not far from the beach, were huge rocks where seals sunned themselves.

Up on the headland, she could see the village itself, a tiny collection of New England-style saltbox houses and clapboard buildings. Mendocino was formerly a fishing village, now a haven for artists, surrounded by some of the most spectacular natural scenery on the magnificent Northern California coast.

When Caroline had gone there before, just after Edward told her he was in love with another woman, she had found it a peaceful place, soothing to the spirit. This time, however, she found no ease for her intense pain. Again and again, she asked herself how Rafe could have done what he did to her—and why. She didn't understand it. She only knew that for the second time in her life she had trusted him with her heart, and he'd broken it.

She was twice a fool, and it was time she put him behind her forever. Only she couldn't. He haunted her day and night, leaving her yearning for the touch and taste and feel of him.

She wasn't sure how she would do it, but somehow she would survive without him. She had done it before when she was much younger and weaker, and she could certainly do it now when she was a mature woman, in control of her life.

But she knew her life would never be the same.

As she looked out at the ocean, she wasn't sure if it was spray from the surf or tears that stung her eyes. Then a seal poked his glistening black nose above the water and eyed her curiously. When he decided she was harmless, he began diving and rolling and splashing about in the surf. He was so cute, Caroline found herself smiling at him, and her eyes cleared.

Feeling a little better, she decided it was time to go back to the inn and have dinner. Maybe she would actually be able to enjoy the food, instead of swallowing it without even tasting it.

As she turned back the way she'd come from the village, she saw someone walking down the beach toward her. In the off-season, there were few tourists, and she'd had the beach to herself. She was glad she was leaving now, because she didn't feel like having company.

Looking away from the oncoming man, she plodded through the sand. Then, when she was nearly abreast of him, she glanced up and froze in her tracks.

Rafe.

She was too stunned to even speak.

His suit was wrinkled, his hair windblown. He looked exhausted and haggard—and wonderful. But she steeled herself against him. It didn't matter why he was there. She wanted nothing to do with him.

"Caroline, I . . ."

She started to walk past him determinedly.

Reaching out, his hand grabbed her shoulder and turned her to face him. "You've got to listen to me."

"No!" she exploded. Pain and anger welled up within her, and she felt like a volcano about to erupt. "I don't know how you found me. . . ."

"Marcia told me where you were."

For a moment she looked stunned. That was a betrayal, and she didn't understand it. But she forced herself to go on, her voice bitter, "It doesn't matter how you persuaded her to tell you. I know how persuasive you can be when you go after something. But I won't talk to you. I want nothing to do with you ever again!"

"I love you, Caroline."

The words brought her up short. They were the very last she expected to hear from him. But she didn't for one moment believe them.

"On your lips, those words are obscene. Now, let me go."

"Look at this!"

He pulled a small book from inside his jacket and held it out toward her.

She was about to push it away, when she saw the title. *Sonnets From the Portuguese*. The famous collection of love poems from Elizabeth Barrett Browning to her husband, Robert Browning. The very book Caroline had given Rafe so many years ago.

For an instant she hesitated, then slowly reached out and took it from his outstretched hand. At the same time he let go of her shoulder. But he continued to watch her intently.

She opened the book and saw the inscription she'd written to him—*To Rafe, with all my love, forever, Caroline.*

"You kept it," she whispered.

He nodded. "Even when I thought you hated me, I couldn't bring myself to destroy it."

Her brown eyes were round with surprise. "Hated you? Why would you think that?"

From his pocket, he took out the note and handed it to her.

"This is why."

She scanned it quickly, and when she looked back up at him again, she was thoroughly confused. "But this isn't the note I wrote to you."

"I know that now. I didn't know it for twenty-five years."

As she stood there, thunderstruck, he went on carefully, "You gave my father another note, didn't you?"

She nodded. "I asked him to give it to you because my parents wouldn't let me call you or see you. And they monitored my mail. Your father was reluctant to take it, but I finally persuaded him to."

"I think he gave the note to your father."

"But why would he do that?"

"He was worried about what your father might do to him, that's why. Your father was an important man in town. My family was nothing. My father was afraid I would end up in jail."

"You might have," Caroline whispered. "My father kept me from seeing you by threatening to have you arrested."

He smiled down at her gently. "I know."

Then he went on soberly, "I tried to see you, to ask you to marry me."

"You did?" She was stunned by this announcement.

"Yes, I did. I loved you, Caroline. I wanted you, and I wanted your child."

"But when I told you I was pregnant, you were certainly less than thrilled!"

"I was scared stiff, Caroline. We were both seventeen, just out of high school. I worked for minimum wage at a garage. I didn't know how I was going to support a wife and child. It would be really rough, I knew, and I wanted more than that for you and our child. You were used to being well off, and I didn't want to drag you down."

"Drag me down? Oh, Rafe, I wouldn't have cared how rough it was. As long as we were together."

"I know, love, I know. Marcia told me how you stuck it out through a very tough time, on your own. I know you would have stuck by me, too."

"But, Rafe, where did you get this note?"

"From your father."

"You mean . . . he wrote this?"

"Yes. To persuade me that you hated me. It worked." He shook his head slowly. "The terrible thing is, I think both our fathers thought they were doing the right thing."

"Oh, my God. And for all these years you thought that I didn't love you after all. You thought I gave up our child."

"And you thought I didn't want that child—or you."

"Oh, Rafe!"

She flung her arms around him, still clutching the book. But the note she let flutter to the ground. She didn't ever want to look at it again.

He held her so tightly she could hardly breathe, but it didn't matter. All that mattered was that they were together now, as they should have been twenty-five years earlier. As his lips brushed her hair, he whispered words of love and apology, begging her to forgive him for hurting her so.

She smiled up at him through her tears and whispered in a choked voice, "It's all right, love. It's finally all right."

"But, Caroline, I wasn't there for you when you needed me! All the lost years with Marina. My God, I just met her for the first time this morning."

"You met her? Where?"

"At your house. I've practically been camped out there, waiting for you to come back. I couldn't go through with it, you see. Even before I learned the truth about what happened back then, I faced the fact that I loved you and couldn't let you go. Marina came to see you, and we talked briefly. As soon as I saw her, I knew."

Caroline's eyes shone with pride. "Yes, she's you all over again, isn't she? And with your pride and temper, as well. Did you . . . did you tell her about us?"

"No. Obviously, she didn't know I was her father. But I want to tell her, Caroline."

"Yes, we should tell her—together."

"Does she care a great deal for Edward?"

"No. They were never really close, but she was shaken by the divorce. This will be hard for her to accept, Rafe."

"I know. But we'll work it out somehow. We can work out anything if we're together."

His face grew hard as he went on, "If it wasn't for your father and mine, we could have been together all this time. I could have watched my daughter grow up."

Putting her fingers to his lips, she whispered, "Hush, now, love. Let's waste no more time on bitterness. We've found each other again. And we have the rest of our lives to make up for what we've lost."

He pulled her into a tight embrace, and his voice was almost desperately fierce. "I'll never let you go again. Never!"

The sharpness of his tone startled the seal out in the water. He dived beneath the surface, then came up again a moment later. Now the shouting was over and the people on the beach were walking away. His whiskers bristled with relief.

Everything was all right.

OFFICIAL SWEEPSTAKES INFORMATION

1. **NO PURCHASE NECESSARY.** To enter, complete the official entry/order form. Be sure to indicate whether or not you wish to take advantage of our subscription offer.

2. Entry blanks have been pre-selected for the prizes offered. Your response will be checked to see if you are a winner. In the event that these are not claimed, a random drawing will be held from all entries received to award not less than $150,000 in prizes. This is in addition to any free, surprise or mystery gifts which might be offered. Versions of this sweepstakes with different prizes will appear in Torstar Ltd. mailings and their affiliates. Winners selected will receive the prize offered in their sweepstakes insert.

3. This promotion is being conducted under the supervision of Marden-Kane, an independent judging organization. By entering the sweepstakes, each entrant accepts and agrees to be bound by these rules and the decisions of the judges which shall be final and binding. Odds of winning in the random drawing are dependent upon the total number of entries received. Taxes, if any, are the sole responsibility of the prize winners. Prizes are non-transferable. All entries must be received by August 31, 1986.

4. This sweepstakes package offers:

1, Grand Prize	Cruise around the world on the QEII	$100,000 total value
4, First Prizes	Set of matching pearl necklace and earrings	$ 20,000 total value
10, Second Prizes	Romantic Weekend in Bermuda	$ 15,000 total value
25, Third Prizes	Designer Luggage	$ 10,000 total value
200, Fourth Prizes	$25 Gift Certificate	$ 5,000 total value
		$150,000

   Winners may elect to receive the cash equivalent for the prizes offered.

5. This offer is open to residents of the U.S. and Canada, 18 years and older, except employees of Torstar Ltd., its affiliates, subsidiaries, Marden-Kane and all other agencies and persons connected with conducting this sweepstakes. All Federal, State and local laws apply. Void in the province of Quebec and wherever prohibited or restricted by law. Winners will be notified by mail and may be required to execute an affidavit of eligibility and release which must be returned within 14 days after notification. Canadian winners will be required to answer a skill testing question. Winners consent to the use of their names, photograph and/or likeness for advertising and publicity purposes in conjunction with this and similar promotions without additional compensation. One prize per family or household.

6. For a list of our most current prize winners, send a stamped, self-addressed envelope to: WINNERS LIST, c/o Marden-Kane, P.O. Box 10404, Long Island City, New York 11101.

Silhouette Special Edition

COMING NEXT MONTH

NOBODY'S FOOL—Renee Roszel
Cara never minded a little fun and games . . . but only on her own terms. So when businessman Martin Dante challenged her to a nine-mile race, she feared the results would be "winner take all!"

THE SECURITY MAN—Dixie Browning
Though Valentine had survived both a bad marriage and an accident that had left her widowed, she wasn't quite ready for her new handsome neighbor. Val couldn't risk loving, but with Cody it was all too tempting.

YESTERDAY'S LIES—Lisa Jackson
Iron willed and proud, Tory was not about to be manipulated, especially not by Trask McFadden. The attractive young senator had deceived her in the past—could he convince her that this time his love was real?

AFTER DARK—Elaine Camp
Sebastian was a man haunted by the past. Everly was a woman determined to control her future. Now he was back to reclaim her heart. Could she be convinced of the healing power of love?

MAGIC SEASON—Anne Lacey
Independence was her trademark and Game Warden Laura Marchand kept her image with spit and polish. But sportsman Ryan D'Arco was hunting her territory and was about to capture her heart.

LESSONS LEARNED—Nora Roberts
Juliet could smell success when she was assigned to do the publicity tour for Italy's most famous chef. But Carlo distracted her with his charms, setting his romantic recipes simmering in her heart.

AVAILABLE NOW:

CHEROKEE FIRE
Gena Dalton

A FEW SHINING HOURS
Jeanne Stephens

PREVIEW OF PARADISE
Tracy Sinclair

A PASSIONATE ILLUSION
Tory Cates

ALL MY LOVE, FOREVER
Pamela Wallace

FORWARD PASS
Brooke Hastings

AMERICAN TRIBUTE

Where a man's dreams count for more than his parentage...

Look for these upcoming titles under the Special Edition American Tribute banner.

CHEROKEE FIRE
Gena Dalton #307—May 1986
It was Sabrina Dante's silver spoon that
Cherokee cowboy Jarod Redfeather couldn't
trust. The two lovers came from opposite
worlds, but Jarod's Indian heritage taught
them to overcome their differences.

NOBODY'S FOOL
Renee Roszel #313—June 1986
Everyone bet that Martin Dante and Cara
Torrence would get together. But Martin
wasn't putting any money down, and Cara
was out to prove that she was nobody's fool.

MISTY MORNINGS, MAGIC NIGHTS
Ada Steward #319—July 1986
The last thing Carole Stockton wanted was to
fall in love with another politician, especially
Donnelly Wakefield. But under a blanket of
secrecy, far from the campaign spotlights,
their love became a powerful force.

AMERICAN TRIBUTE

American Tribute titles now available:

RIGHT BEHIND THE RAIN
Elaine Camp #301—April 1986
The difficulty of coping with her brother's
death brought reporter Raleigh Torrence
to the office of Evan Younger, a police
psychologist. He helped her to deal with
her feelings and emotions, including love.

THIS LONG WINTER PAST
Jeanne Stephens #295—March 1986
Detective Cody Wakefield checked out
Assistant District Attorney Liann McDowell,
but only in his leisure time. For it was the
danger of Cody's job that caused Liann to
shy away.

LOVE'S HAUNTING REFRAIN
Ada Steward #289—February 1986
For thirty years a deep dark secret kept them
apart—King Stockton made his millions while
his wife, Amelia, held everything together.
Now could they tell their secret, could they
admit their love?

Take 4 Silhouette
Special Edition novels
FREE
and preview future books in your home for 15 days!

When you take advantage of this offer, you get 4 Silhouette Special Edition® novels FREE and without obligation. Then you'll also have the opportunity to preview 6 brand-new books —delivered right to your door for a FREE 15-day examination period—as soon as they are published.

When you decide to keep them, you pay just $1.95 each ($2.50 each in Canada) *with no shipping, handling, or other charges of any kind!*

Romance *is* alive, well and flourishing in the moving love stories of Silhouette Special Edition novels. They'll awaken your desires, enliven your senses, and leave you tingling all over with excitement...and the first 4 novels are yours to keep. You can cancel at any time.

As an added bonus, you'll also receive a FREE subscription to the Silhouette Books Newsletter as long as you remain a member. Each issue is filled with news on upcoming books, interviews with your favorite authors, even their favorite recipes.

To get your 4 FREE books, fill out and mail the coupon today!

Silhouette Special Edition®

Silhouette Books, 120 Brighton Rd., P.O. Box 5084, Clifton, NJ 07015-5084